BE
WRC _ ⌐ꓤＵＩＨＥＲ

Determined to find her inner sex diva, Melina Parker enlists her childhood friend, Max Dalton, to tutor her after hours. Instead, she ends up in the wrong bed and gets a lesson in passion from Max's twin brother, Rhys Dalton, a man Melina's always secretly wanted but never thought she could have.

This #1 Bestselling Contemporary Romance is rated HHH ("Heat, Heart & HEA") and involves a bed mix-up, hot identical twins, sex lessons, naughty word games, light restraint, a shy sex bomb who's afraid she's boring and a playboy hero determined to prove she's got everything he'll ever need.

BEDDING
The Wrong Brother

BEDDING THE BACHELORS, BOOK ONE

by

VIRNA DEPAUL

Bedding The Wrong Brother
Copyright © 2012 by Virna DePaul

This is a work of fiction. Names, characters, places, brands, media, and incidents are either the product of the author's imagination or are used fictitiously.

PROLOGUE

Dalton's Magic Rule #1:
Never reveal your secrets.

"Hey, Ladybug."

Fourteen-year-old Melina Parker's hand jerked at the sound of Rhys Dalton's voice, causing the lizard in her palm to scamper away. Standing, she frowned to hide the sudden flight of butterflies in her stomach. "Darn it, Rhys. It took me almost an hour to get that one to come to me."

Rhys, who even at sixteen towered over Melina's petite frame, rolled his eyes. He was an identical twin, and it was hard for Melina to believe there were two gorgeous guys with that same shade of honey-colored hair and light green eyes walking the earth.

"Your mom said to tell you to stay clean." The left side of his mouth quirked up, revealing the slightest hint of a dimple. "Guess it's too late for that."

Melina glanced down at the dust covering her jeans.

Grimacing, she slapped at the dirt and groaned. "She's going to kill me. She's already mad that I wouldn't wear the dress she bought me. You should have seen it, Rhys. It had polka dots. I mean, me in *polka dots*. Can you imagine?"

"Oh, come on, it makes sense. Plus, I think you'd be cute in a dress."

At the quiet words, Melina's head jerked up. He couldn't have meant—

No, of course not. He'd been so distant lately. He wasn't even looking at her. Instead, he was staring down at a playing card in his hands, folding it. Nothing strange about that. Like their parents, Rhys and his twin brother, Max, were always fiddling with some kind of magic trick. He was particularly fond of making coins disappear. Sometimes she wished he could make her crush on him disappear just as easily, but first she'd have to admit it to him. That was so never going to happen. She'd seen the types of girls he and Max were attracted to, and plain, chubby tomboys need not apply.

At least he didn't call her "Four-eyed Porker Parker" the way some of the boys at school did. In fact, when Rhys had heard Scott Thompson called her that, he'd tracked Scott down and given him a warning. Now whenever Melina got close, Scott couldn't get away from her fast enough.

Nudging her glasses in place, she moved closer, trying to see what Rhys was doing. "Um. So, have you heard from Max?"

His hands paused briefly before continuing. "Just that he doesn't hate football camp nearly as much as he thought he would. Might have something to do with the girls camp next door."

She snickered. "Bet you're wishing you'd gone to camp when you'd had the chance, huh?"

"Nope."

"Why not?"

His gaze met hers. Unlike Max's, Rhys's pupils had a slight amber ring around them. She'd read somewhere that differing eye color in identical twins was extremely rare. The subtle difference fit Rhys's personality. While Max was almost always carefree and playful, Rhys had a quiet calmness about him—as if part of his mind was someplace else, someplace no one else could go.

He shrugged. "Time at home is rare. You know that."

Melina nodded. She did. It was the hardest thing about being friends with the Dalton twins: the amount of time she had to spend missing them. Unless Rhys's folks were working up a new act, like now, they spent their time traveling and performing. Still, despite having to be schooled on the road by tutors, Rhys and Max always seemed to enjoy going to new places. She certainly envied their chance to see more than this small, university town she called home.

"Poor baby," she teased, plucking a blade of grass from the ground and twirling it. "Getting to see the world with your famous parents must be a drag, huh?"

He frowned, then shook his head. "No, you're right. It's great." He thrust his hand toward her. "Here. To replace the one I scared away."

Dropping the blade of grass, she reached out and took the card. Looking down at it, she gasped. He'd folded the card into a shape that clearly resembled a lizard, with one spade as its eye. A smile split her face, and she actually squealed. "It's so cute!"

She looked up, happy to see that his frown had disappeared. A hank of hair had fallen over his eyes, and her fingers itched to push it back. She wouldn't have thought twice about it if he'd been Max, but with Rhys? She couldn't risk revealing how she felt about him. Next thing she knew, he'd pat her on the head and stop talking to her altogether, and that would kill her.

He shoved his hands in his pockets and shrugged again. "I got this book from the library—"

A movement behind his shoulder made her eyes widen. "Max?" She looked at Rhys, whose expression stiffened. "It's Max!"

Running past Rhys, she threw herself at Max. He laughed and lifted her, twirling her around before setting her on her feet. Even to an outsider, the differences between him and his brother would be obvious now. He was tanner, and his hair had grown longer, almost touching his shoulders. She reached out and flipped it. "What's with the girly hair?"

He narrowed his eyes and flicked a finger over her nose. "Still playing in the dirt, are you?"

She slapped his hand away. "You're home early. Rhys said you were having fun at camp."

"I was. But I wanted to see what Mom and Dad were up to with the act. They're really pushing for something unique for the European tour. Your parents are here helping them?"

"Every day for the past week. Some kind of mechanical thingy."

Max grinned and flung an arm around her shoulder. "Cool. Let's go check it out."

"Okay. But first look at what Rhys made me." She lifted up the paper lizard even as she turned to Rhys. "It's so cool. Rhys, let's—"

Rhys walked past her, nodding at his brother and slapping him on the shoulder. "Come on, dude. You're gonna love it. It's huge. I mean—"

As they walked in front of her, the two of them laughing and shoving, Melina frowned. She watched them, the easy way they had with each other, and hesitated. They'd be back on the road in another few weeks, and then it would be just her and her parents in their quiet little house, all of their noses immersed in books. No one to call her Ladybug or practice tricks on.

No one to dream about.

Which was silly, anyway. Her parents said things came to fruition through research and application, not dreaming. And they were right about everything.

Except polka dot dresses, she amended.

With a sigh, she carefully pocketed the paper lizard and scrambled to catch up with them. "Hey, guys! Wait up!"

1

Dalton's Magic Rule #2:
Continually challenge yourself.

"Listen to this," Lucy Conrad said, waving Melina's magazine like a red flag. "98.9 percent of all women sometimes wish their lovers would just grab them, throw them down and fuck the holy hell out of them." Tossing the magazine on the sofa, she pointed a finger in Melina's direction, her short and spiky red hair fairly vibrating. "You know what that means, don't you?"

"That women like to feel wanted?" Melina guessed, handing Lucy a pint of Ben & Jerry's Cherry Garcia ice cream before dropping into the chair across from her. Sitting cross-legged, Melina adjusted her glasses, then scooped out a bite of Chunky Monkey from her own carton. It had been exactly seven days since she'd allowed herself this taste of heaven. When the cold confection touched her tongue, she closed her eyes in appreciation. "Hmm," she purred. "Gotta love Girls' Night In."

"You can say that again." The soft but impassioned reply came from Grace Sinclair, who sat in a chair next to Melina. Melina held out her spoon and Grace delicately tapped it with her own. Grace, a career counselor in the university's humanities department, was class and calmness personified. While Lucy was Cherry Garcia—cherry ice cream with cherries and fudge flakes—Grace was Ben & Jerry's Crème Brûlée—sweet custard ice cream with a caramelized sugar swirl. Blond and willowy with cool porcelain skin, Grace spoke with just a hint of a Southern drawl. "All we need is a Viggo Mortensen movie and I'd be halfway to heaven."

"You already tried that, remember? Even with Viggo's voice playing in the background, you couldn't get off."

Grace squinted at Lucy while waving her spoon. "Now don't you go blaming that on Viggo. I could hardly hear him with all the grunting noises Phillip was making." Grace wrinkled her nose. "I swear, the man had the nicest table manners, but in bed…" She gave a mock shudder.

Melina giggled as Lucy thumped on the magazine she'd been reading from.

"Seriously," Lucy insisted. "This does not mean women like to feel wanted. It means they settle for fantasies instead of focusing on what they really want at the beginning of a relationship. Which is exactly what you're doing, Melina."

Sighing, Melina forced a smile. The last thing she wanted was to have another argument with Lucy about

Professor Jamie Whitcomb. Unfortunately, despite the dusting of freckles that made Lucy look more like one of her students than a tenured professor, Lucy was a bulldog when it came to protecting her friends—even from themselves. "And exactly what should I be focusing on?" she asked.

"Passion," Lucy fired back.

Of course. Passion. Lucy's favorite word. "And by passion, you mean…"

"Pure, animalistic chemistry. The kind that makes you want to rip each other's clothes off and do it against a tree if you have to. The kind of passion you don't feel for Jamie."

The kind of passion she'd never felt for any man, Melina thought. Any man except Rhys, that is. But thinking of Rhys only made her sad, and being sad while she ate Ben & Jerry's was just wrong. "Ahh," Melina said softly, trying not to sound too bitter. "You mean the kind of mutual passion that leads to love and lifelong happiness and is about as real as unicorns or flying dragons."

"Rarity isn't the same as fantasy," Lucy exclaimed. She stood, her face all flushed and her hands gesturing wildly. "That's what women have been taught nowadays. That passion and true love and friendship, all rolled into one, is impossible. So they settle."

"Lucy does have a point," Grace admitted. "Passion must be a basic female need. Otherwise, why would such a huge percentage of women be craving it?"

"Maybe," Melina said, trying to be the voice of

reason, "because 98.9 percent of guys aren't the throw-a-woman-on-the-ground type." Her eyes automatically shifted to the pictures of Max and Rhys on her bookshelves. She had a feeling they were the exception, but they didn't exactly represent the average male. "Women want passion, but if it's not in a man's true nature to give it to her, then what's the point in wishing for it? Compatibility. Respect. Even love. That's what matters."

"So then what's with all these?" Lucy pointed to several books on Melina's coffee table. *The Joy of Sex* rested prominently on top of the stack.

Melina shrugged prosaically, pretty sure Lucy already knew the answer. "Guys like sex. Jamie's a guy. Thus, part of getting and keeping Jamie is giving him sex."

And not just any kind of sex, Melina thought. Mind-blowing, can't-live-without-it, I'll-never-look-at-another-woman-for-fear-you-won't-give-it-to-me-again sex. The kind of sex she apparently didn't know how to provide, but was going to master this time even if it meant renting every porno she could find on the Internet.

"You like sex, too," Grace pointed out. "Do you factor into this equation at all?"

"Of course, I do. I have no doubt that Jamie can give me what I want."

Lucy harrumphed and narrowed her eyes at her. "Well, I'm glad your wants are still in the picture. At least Brian didn't totally squash your sexual confidence when he hooked up with his little co-ed."

No, Melina thought, he'd squashed her confidence

long before then. Every time he'd hinted she needed to lose a few pounds. And he hadn't been the only one of her boyfriends prone to doing that. But insecurities aside, she knew she was healthy and reasonably attractive. That just wasn't enough for some men. The key was finding the man who'd love her for who she was.

And who she could *learn* to be in bed.

"True passion isn't about technique, Melina," Lucy insisted. "You can't manufacture it by reading about it."

Melina nodded. "I get that. But I've never been overly passionate, anyway. After Brian, I was sure I was through with men for good. But then Jamie approached me. He's smart and kind and funny. I think I could be happy with him." She heard the hesitation in her voice but charged on. "I just need a little extra insurance that I can make him happy, too."

Snorting, Lucy shook her head. "If you're talking about making him happy in bed, there's no such thing as insurance. You'll just have to take the plunge, so to speak."

"Not necessarily," Grace drawled. "As my mama always said, practice makes perfect, right?"

Lucy's brows furrowed, while Melina gave an internal groan. She recognized the challenge behind that drawl. For a woman who was so contained, Grace could throw down a challenge like nobody's business. Worse yet, she'd be the first to take one up, which made Lucy and Melina hard-pressed to turn one down themselves.

Melina turned to Grace, whose impish smile was

unmistakable. "And just who are you suggesting I practice with?" she asked.

In sync, all of their gazes moved to the same shelf of pictures. Melina's stomach clenched even as she zoomed in on the most recent addition. Max and Rhys both looked impossibly handsome in black tuxedos. She'd taken it at the IBM Magic Convention in Vegas last year, right after they'd beat out Chris Angel and Lance Burton for Best Stage Magician of the Year. Of course, in the picture each had an arm around his date: Max, a tall, leggy redhead, and Rhys, a stacked brunette whose boobs were almost spilling out of her plunging neckline.

Melina dropped her gaze to her ice cream container. Unless they had begun manufacturing implants, she'd bet that brunette had never heard of Ben and Jerry. Suddenly feeling as if every bite of ice cream had gone straight to her hips and thighs, she set the carton aside.

"Rhys?" she asked doubtfully. "I said I need insurance I can satisfy Jamie, and you want me to drive head-on into a brick wall. Rhys is in a whole different league than Jamie."

"Exactly," Grace replied. "You want him, yet you've let fear hold you back. You're turning twenty-eight in a week, Melina. Why not overcome two fears at the same time? Prove to yourself you can satisfy a man like Rhys, and you'll necessarily prove you can satisfy someone like Jamie, as well."

"You're wicked," Lucy breathed, sounding utterly impressed.

Grace bowed in acknowledgment.

Melina shook her head and held up her hands. "Just hold on. You're assuming I can satisfy Rhys. How likely is that? I couldn't even keep Brian satisfied in bed, and he'd only been with two other women. With all the women Rhys has had…" Melina swallowed hard, the very thought of all those women causing an ache of mammoth proportions in her chest.

"All the more reason to ask him. Think what a fabulous teacher he'd be," Grace urged.

But Melina was already shaking her head again. Defiantly, she picked up her ice cream container and took a fortifying bite. "No way," she mumbled around the spoon. "Rhys doesn't even like me anymore. We haven't talked for months."

Obviously, he was too preoccupied with the showgirl-type women he was often photographed with to have time for an old friend. Of course, he'd proved to her long ago that nailing the hottest chick was more important than friendship. Her mistake had been in thinking it was a one-time thing. "Forget it. I'm not asking Rhys for anything."

Her tone brooked no argument, or so she thought. After a few seconds, Lucy shot her a sideways glance. "Okay, so if not Rhys, what about Max?"

Melina choked, coughed, and wheezed, "Max?"

"Of course," Grace said, nodding and smiling in delight. "He has even more experience than Rhys. And she's completely comfortable with him."

"Not that comfortable," Melina interjected, only to be

ignored.

"She trusts him," Lucy agreed. "He's a hottie. They've already kissed once—"

"That was almost twelve years ago and he felt sorry for me—"

"And he's flying in for her birthday. He's perfect."

"Perfect," Grace echoed. "Talk about sexual empowerment."

Melina's gaze bounced back and forth between her friends as her mind frantically tried to come up with a reason why sleeping with Max was a bad idea.

She couldn't come up with one.

Still, it would be humiliating to cave so soon. Narrowing her eyes, she asked, "And exactly what sexual empowerment issue would you two be addressing during my crash course in satisfying a man?" She looked over at Grace, who'd started to braid a strip of her long pale hair. "Grace?"

Grace stopped braiding, bit her lip, then shrugged, her mouth twisting into a sardonic smile. "No point in denying my greatest fear, now is there? My birthday's two weeks after yours, so I'll try to find the man I fear doesn't exist: the man who can get me off. I'm sure it will just lead to another weekend of frustration, but as long as I can keep my vibrator handy, I'm willing to suffer for the cause."

Although she felt herself softening, Melina didn't reach out to her friend. This challenge had been Grace's idea. Maybe she needed it more than Melina did. She hadn't dated in almost a year, convinced that if she couldn't even attain pleasure with a man, there was no point in putting up with one. Lucy, on the other hand, put so much stock on pleasure that she often put up with a man's failings longer than she should. Melina turned to her friend, keeping her face impassive despite the scowl on Lucy's face. Lucy's birthday wasn't for a few months, but it was a big one, the big 3-0.

"I should get a pass on this one," Lucy said. "I'm fearless when it comes to sex, you know that. I've tried everything there is to try. There's no reason—"

"You fear intimacy," Grace said gently. "You only date jerks, guys who are never going to commit to you—"

"Just because I happen to love brooding, creative men with an edge does not mean I fear intimacy," Lucy protested.

"It's one weekend, Lucy. One weekend with a nice guy you normally wouldn't give a second look," Melina clarified.

"A nice guy?" Lucy looked outraged. "Oh, sure. For your birthday weekend, you get to ask a hot friend to show you everything he knows in bed. Grace gets to have someone pleasure her for two days straight or die trying. What do I get? A nice guy who probably doesn't know a cock-ring from a cockatoo." She held up a hand to forestall Melina's response. "But fine. If you two can do it, then so can I."

Lucy paused and smiled sweetly, which, from her, was the equivalent of a big, flashing "danger" sign. "I call the stakes. Anyone who puts their plan in motion and sticks with it the entire birthday weekend, regardless of the results, gets a full day of pampering at Silk Spa. Anyone who chickens out has to get up in front of my Women's Studies 101 class and explain why. In excruciating detail. And answer questions afterwards."

Lucy stuck out her hand, palm down. After a brief hesitation, Grace placed her hand gently on top of it. Melina's hands curled into fists. Her gaze landed on the magazine that Lucy had been reading, the one with the sex survey she'd read through earlier. She'd committed one paragraph to memory: "Of those people who are very satisfied with their sex lives, ninety percent are also very satisfied with their marriage or committed relationship overall. The less sexually satisfied people reported being, the less satisfied they were with their marriage or partnership."

It sounded so simple, she thought. Keep a man satisfied and he'd be less likely to stray, right? Continually blow a man's mind in bed, and he'd be yours for life. In that way, men weren't unlike the bugs Melina studied: give them what they wanted and they'd give back to you.

With Max as her teacher, she'd learn to keep a man sexually satisfied. And she was an excellent student. She'd just never given that particular skill her total focus. Once she did, how hard could it be?

She shakily laid her hand on Grace's.

She'd never have Rhys. Maybe being with Max was the next best thing. One thing was for sure, though. Given the parameters that Lucy had set, none of them was backing out of this challenge.

* * *

"So, when do you leave for Sacramento?" Rhys called to Max. He tried to sound nonchalant, focusing his attention on lifting Laura's supple, feminine leg and placing the delicate ankle in the leather restraint. He refused to look at Max, instead tugging the leather to make sure the restraint held firm. Then he did the same thing with Laura's other leg, ending with a playful growl that caused her to giggle.

Satisfied that she was now fully restrained, he continued to play his part, absently dragging his fingertips up the inside of her gently curved calf and then her soft, pale thigh, continuing the journey over a lush hip, nipped waist, generous breast and upraised arm until he grasped the single restraint that bound her two fragile wrists together. Max still hadn't answered.

Standing directly in front of Laura, his feet braced apart, his chest just brushing her magnificent breasts, he turned to look at his brother. "Max?"

His brother wasn't paying any attention to him. Instead, he was staring at the floor, his brows flexed. Rhys sighed, released the leather restraint that was suspended from the contraption on a chain, and smiled at Laura. "Give me a second?"

She chewed her gum and winked. "I'm not going anywhere."

Rhys marveled at the huskiness of her voice. Although she was dressed in a modest leotard and tights rather than the skimpy sequined outfit she wore during a performance, everything from her voice to her polished toes was a walking wet dream. It wasn't necessarily an act, either. Even when she was lecturing her teenage son about doing his homework, she still managed to sound like a sex phone operator. Striding toward Max, who leaned against the stage-left wall, Rhys rolled his shoulders and tried to suppress his impatience.

It figured that the moment their dream was within reach, Max would get into one of his brooding moods. Normally, Rhys could tolerate and compensate for Max's moods, just like Max did for him, but with the recent back-to-back rehearsals combined with the time he was spending working the kinks out of the Dalton Brothers' newest stage trick—the most spectacular one to date—his tolerance was spent. Next week's show had to go off without a hitch. Add to this stress the fact that Melina's birthday was coming up? Exhausted didn't even begin to describe how he was feeling.

"Max? Max!"

Max blinked and straightened, his faraway gaze focusing on Rhys and then on Laura, who still hung in the customized apparatus behind them. He raked a hand through his already disheveled hair and jerked his chin at Rhys. "Did you need me to test out those restraints now?"

Rhys smiled tightly. "I'm sure Laura can wait until her hands go numb if you need a few more minutes in la-la land."

Shaking his head, Max strode to Laura. "Sorry about that, babe. I was just thinking."

Behind him, Rhys snorted. "I thought we agreed that until we land the contract with Seven Seas, you'd let me do the thinking while you focused on flexing your muscles and shaking your ass at the audience."

"What would it matter if it was my ass or yours? The audience rarely knows the difference."

Rhys hung his head. When Max was right, he was right. The whole mystique around the Dalton Twins' Magic Show was that the audience knew the magician performing that night was an identical twin; they just didn't know which one. Not until the end of the show. The problem was that he was more and more content to let Max be the performer so that he could do what he liked best: focus on managing the act and inventing new tricks. He'd had to step up the number of his own performances or risk losing the mystery hook altogether. Plus, once they unveiled their new trick, Rhys wouldn't get a reprieve for a good long time. Floating Metamorphosis would be spectacular only if the audience saw both Dalton twins on stage at the same time.

After tugging on the restraints like a volunteer from the audience would do, Max nodded his head at Lou, one of the backstage assistants. As Lou began to loosen the restraints, Max absently patted Laura's hip. In response, Laura blew Max an air kiss.

Laura and Lou left the stage, but not before Laura shot

a seductive backward glance at Max. Suddenly, the fact that the two of them had sauntered into practice half-an-hour late, their hair mussed and looking like they'd barely slept, took on new meaning. Rhys glowered at his brother. "Jesus, Max, you just couldn't keep your hands off, could you? Not even for a few weeks?"

Max shrugged and held out his palms in a "what of it?" gesture.

"What happens when you piss her off and she quits the night of a show? Are you trying to screw up everything we've worked for?"

"You're not giving Laura enough credit. She's a big girl. Last night was fun, but she's still got a thing for her ex. She's driving up to see him this weekend. And her son, too, of course."

"That's not the point," Rhys snapped. "I've had to double security since we caught Joey Salvador trying to sneak backstage. Seven Seas is insisting we come up with a G-rated proposal for their family-night performances. And let's not forget that after tonight's show, I'm going to have to get everything packed up and shipped to Reno on my own, while you jet to California for the weekend. Things are crazy enough around here without me having to worry about your sex life, too."

Grim-faced, Max opened his mouth to respond, but a voice offstage stopped him. It was their father. "Boys, your mother's about to have a stroke. Jillian insists we need to shake things up for the Seven Seas folks and replace your black ties and cummerbunds with something that matches the girls' outfits. I think they're getting ready to battle it out. Come quick!"

Forgetting for a moment why he was so pissed, Rhys looked at Max. He was sure his face reflected the same horror that Max's did. Their stage assistants wore shimmery sequined costumes in colors ranging from rose to fuchsia. No matter what Jillian called it, it was still pink to Rhys.

Max cursed. "Are you done flaying me? 'Cause I, for one, don't want to go on stage looking like a pansy."

Rhys swiped his hands over his face before shaking his head. What was the point? Max was just being Max. It wasn't his fault Rhys was wound so tight. Not really. "Fuck. Forget it. I'm just tired. I'll go deal with Jillian." He paused, then muttered, "Tell Melina happy birthday for me."

Rhys hadn't taken more than four steps before Max clapped a hand on his shoulder, yanking him back a step. "Why don't you tell her yourself? I know I haven't been pulling my weight lately. I'll stay. You use my ticket and surprise Melina." Max grinned. "See if she notices the switch this time."

Rhys managed to smile. When they'd been younger, he and Max had played the same stupid games with Melina that they'd played with everyone else. They'd taken turns pretending to be one twin while subtly urging their victims to say something derogatory about the other. Melina was the only one who'd never fallen for it. Not once. She had an uncanny ability to tell them apart, even from a distance. That was one of the things that had drawn him to her in the first place.

It was also why, when he'd found her kissing Max on the night of her sixteenth birthday, there'd been no telling himself she'd really meant to kiss him.

Rhys's smile vanished at the memory. That kiss had interfered with two friendships over the years: his friendship with Melina and his friendship with his brother. Max and Melina's kiss had apparently been a one-time deal, but it had still enflamed the sense of discomfort he'd already felt when they were all together. He'd fought that discomfort for close to ten years by trying to remain Melina's friend. All it had done was make it impossible for him to get over her.

His plan had been working, though. By minimizing their contact over the past two years, he was finally beginning to miss her less. Hell, he could now go hours, days even, without thinking of her, and his focus was exactly where it should be: on his family, their act, and ensuring the continued success of both.

Max gave him a shove. "My ticket's in my dressing room. If you pack now, you can leave right after the show and—"

Shaking his head, Rhys couldn't quite meet his brother's eyes. "I can't," he clipped out. "There's too much to do."

"What's to do? The crew knows how to pack up without us. The Salvador Brothers wouldn't dare show their faces around here again. And as far as Seven Seas' ridiculous request for a kiddie show goes, they can shove it—"

Rhys raised his brows pointedly, causing Max's words to trail off. He grimaced. "Too much?"

"Just a little."

"I can tone it down. I know Melina would love to see you—"

"No," Rhys said, shaking his head again. "You're the one she feels comfortable around. She always has."

"Damn it, Rhys, she's not a kid anymore. And she's had a crush on you for years."

Rhys jerked back as if his brother had hauled off and punched him. He immediately narrowed his eyes in warning. "I'm not a substitute for you or anyone, Max. I never will be."

His brother flushed guiltily. "It was one kiss, and she didn't even initiate it—"

"Yeah, so you told me, but we're talking ancient history. I got over her a long time ago." The two of them, mirror images, stared at each other, and it was Rhys's turn to flush. Unwilling to face his own dishonesty, he stared at the stage floor.

"When did you turn into a liar?" Max asked quietly. "And more importantly, when did you start to think I was an idiot? We work together. We're brothers. You don't think I can read you?"

Rhys's face jerked up. "Yeah, well, maybe that's the problem."

"Now we have a problem?"

"You think you know me, but you don't. Just like you don't really know Melina. If you did, we wouldn't be having this conversation. Even if she did want me for more than your stand-in, I can't give her what she wants any more than you can."

"Speak for yourself." His gaze dropped to Rhys's groin. "Something happen I don't know about?"

"Asshole," Rhys gritted. He reached out and punched Max on the shoulder with a little more force than necessary. "I'm talking about stability. Roots."

His brother rubbed the spot where he'd hit him. "Oh."

"Yeah. Oh. You know she's prime mother material. She's got a job she loves. She wants the white picket fence, two-point-two kids. I can't give that to her."

"Maybe she doesn't know what she wants. Maybe she wants to travel. Going on the road could be an adventure."

"She could travel. She chooses not to. Not even with her parents. Even if she'd consider it, it wouldn't be for the long term. You really think she'd do that to her kids? The childhood we had, Max—" He lifted his arms and encompassed the entire theater in one sweeping motion. "The life we have *now* isn't conventional. It's not what most people want."

"It sounds like maybe it's not what you want anymore. Is that it?"

Unease tickled at his brain. He could feel it. They were about to become big—really big—and he was used to the lifestyle. Maybe at one time he'd wanted something different, but that had been a grass-is-greener-on-the-other-side moment. "Are you kidding? I've never liked traveling as much as you, but if we land this contract with Seven Seas, we'll at least have our own theater. No more moving from one place to another every two weeks. We're at the top of our game. It's what you've always wanted."

"You mean we."

"What?"

Max stared at him. "You mean it's what we've always wanted."

"Sure. You. Mom and Dad. Me. We. That's what I meant."

"Uh-huh."

"Boys!" Their dad poked his head around the corner, his sparse hair sticking up in tufts as if he'd been pulling at it. "Fair warning. I'm not the one who's going to go on stage in sequins."

"I'm coming, Dad." Shaking his head, Rhys began walking backward. "Look, I don't know how we got on this ridiculous topic. Melina and I are friends. I'm happy with the act. Everything's cool." Turning so he wouldn't have to see the doubt on his brother's face any longer, Rhys strode toward backstage. Over his shoulder, he called, "Take her out. Make her feel special. And tell her I'll see her…well, I'll see her sometime."

Rhys forced himself to keep walking despite the little voice in his head screaming that he was a coward. Hell, he wasn't a coward, he was just realistic.

He had his life and Melina had hers. Plus, he'd told Max the truth: Their goals were so far apart they might as well live on opposite ends of the world. Still, he thought with a sigh after opening the door to the costume room, he'd been tempted by Max's offer more than he should have been. Especially because he'd wanted Melina to mistake him for Max.

Just once, he'd have liked Melina to greet him the same way she did Max. With open arms and an open smile instead of a friendly but reserved detachment that always left him wanting more.

2

Dalton's Magic Rule #3:
Learn from those with more experience.

"Teach me how to please a man."

Max, who'd just taken a gulp of his beer, choked on it and kept coughing until Melina rose from her chair and began slapping his back. Putting down the bottle, he raised his hands, wheezed, and gently nudged her away. "I'm fine. I just…I think I misunderstood—"

Face flaming but trying to act nonchalant, Melina returned to the chair next to the sofa, crossed her legs, and smoothed her wool skirt so that it covered her knees. "You heard me right. I want you to teach me how to please a man."

He stared at her with rounded eyes that quickly narrowed. Making a big show of looking around her small, neat living room, he muttered, "Is this a joke? Did Rhys put you up to this?"

She leaned forward and waved her hand in front of his

face, knowing it would annoy him. "Focus, Max. I'm not joking."

Grinning now, Max swatted her hand away and wiggled his eyebrows up and down. "Oh, really? So what, you're suddenly hot for my body? Not that I blame you, but—"

"Will you stop?" she hissed. "I'm being serious here." She yanked her wrist from his grip and stood, turning her back to him even as she hugged her arms close to her chest. Where were her friends and her Ben & Jerry's ice cream when she needed them? Knowing she had no choice, she forced herself to continue. "I-I suck in bed."

The stunned silence behind her was deafening. Embarrassment threatened to swallow her whole, and she had to forcibly stop herself from running into the next room.

"Hey, that can be a good thing," Max joked, but his attempt at humor was obviously strained.

"I'm a lousy lover," she clarified.

Again, that moment of silence.

"Says who?" Max growled.

She studied her fingernails, frowning at how ragged they looked. She'd been chewing on them again. "Lots of people."

"Lots?"

"Okay, not lots. Three. But they would know."

"Three? Hell, Melina, that's not enough to conclude anything. And who said it last? That bastard you broke up with six months ago? For a woman who studies bugs for a living, you sure have a problem recognizing the less evolved of the male species. That guy probably couldn't find a woman's G-spot if I drew him a map."

Melina sighed. Wasn't that the truth? But she had to stay focused. She had it on good authority that Brian's inability to find her G-spot was because she hadn't inspired the search. His new girlfriend had taken great delight in pointing that fact out to her.

"Well, not all men are fortunate to be famous entertainers whose female fans want them to sign their underwear."

She heard Max rise and walk closer to her. "Yeah, it's a tough gig, but someone's gotta do it. And it's their naked bodies they want us to sign, not their underwear. I, of course, am always happy to oblige."

Sniffing, she raised her hand. "Of course. Forgive me."

His arms encircled her from behind. Resting his chin on her head, he just held her. As always, she felt protected in his arms. Sheltered. But there was no zing of desire. None of the heat or shivers that overtook her when Rhys was near. On the plus side, there was no feeling like a moron and running away, either.

Not that it would have made a difference if Max did make her hot. Both Max and Rhys were way out of her league, and neither had ever shown the slightest bit of interest in her anyway. Sure, Max had always flirted and teased. Told her to come see him when she wanted a real man. But she knew, as with everything else with him, it had all been a game.

Unfortunately for him, she was calling his bluff.

"If there were, uh, issues—" He cleared his throat. "They were his fault, Melina, not yours."

She snorted and pulled away. "I wish that were true, but he's not the only boyfriend to tell me I don't know what I'm doing. And according to his new girlfriend, he's the bomb."

He winced. "Please. Don't try to talk modern. It just doesn't work."

"See what I mean?" she pouted. "I can't even talk sexy."

"You don't need to talk sexy. Behind those god-awful glasses," he tapped the top of her wire-rimmed glasses for emphasis "lab coats, and lumpy suits you wear, you are sexy. You just don't go around advertising it."

"Right."

"Melina," he said warningly.

"I'm not putting myself down. I'm not beautiful and don't have the best body in the world, I'm attractive, I dress well—"

His snort was getting rather annoying now.

"—and I'm smart. That counts for something, right?"

"Melina—"

"I'm kind. Loyal. I think I'd make a good mother."

Max's eyes bugged out. "Uh, Melina—"

She put her hands on her hips. "Oh, hush. I'm not asking you to father my child. And you don't have to look so relieved, either. But we both know I'm not a femme fatale. I don't want to be. I just want to get married. Have a family." A big one. She wanted lots of children, not an only child who would grow up lonely and longing for the type of sibling relationship that Max had with Rhys. "I don't want to wither up and die surrounded by a bunch of bugs." She dropped gracelessly onto her coach and leaned her head back against the cushion.

His expression grew suspicious. "Is this about your biological clock? Honey, you're still young. There's plenty of time for you to start a family."

When she didn't answer, he dropped down next to her and took her hands. "I thought you liked your bugs," Max said quietly. "Are you that unhappy? Why didn't you tell me?"

She shook her head. "I love my job, but I...but I want to be—" Her voice hitched. "I want to be loved. I want someone to love me."

"Your parents love you. Rhys and I, we love you, Melina."

"My parents and you, maybe. Rhys, I'm not so sure of anymore. And anyway, it's not enough. I want a partner."

"But you're talking sex. Mechanics. Not love."

"One leads to the other," she insisted. "With guys, sex comes first, then emotion, right?"

He looked like he wanted the ground to open up and swallow him. "Well, I guess. To some—"

"To you, right?"

"But I'm not the one you want to make fall in love with you." He said it hesitantly, as if he wasn't sure what her answer would be.

"No. But you'd certainly be demanding. In bed, I mean."

He raked a hand though his golden hair. "Jesus, Melina—"

"I'm just saying…" she soothed.

"What's causing all this? You got your eye on someone specific?"

Her fingers plucked at the corded edge of one of the sofa cushions. Despite Lucy's fervent belief that she'd be settling with Jamie, there was something about the man that called to her. A sort of offbeat humor. A serious stare that pierced you and made you wonder what he was thinking. And whether he was thinking about you. The way Rhys's stare did. But unlike Rhys, he'd expressed interest in her. Asked her out for drinks after the conference next weekend. And she wasn't going to mess up her opportunity with him.

Not this time. "Sort of."

"'Sort of' is a wimpy answer."

She pounded the sofa cushion with her fist. "Okay, I do."

"Let me guess. He's an academic?"

"Well, of course. The sex thing is necessary in the beginning—"

"And in the middle and end," Max said drolly.

"—but after that, we need commonality to build on. I mean, he's not just smart. He's sexy, too. And he's interested in me. There's a conference next week that we're going to be presenting at—"

Max eyes widened in that expression of disbelief again. "You're presenting at a conference? Since when? The last time you tried speaking at a public event, you almost passed out."

"Thank you for that reminder," she gritted out, but without much heat. He was right. She didn't do well in the spotlight. At the workshop Max was talking about, she'd stepped up to the podium only to become paralyzed with terror. She'd morphed from confident scientist into Cindy Brady, staring at a blinking red camera light despite the audience surrounding her. It wasn't an experience she'd ever sought to repeat again. That's why she'd chosen research in the safety and anonymity of her lab. That's what she was used to. That's what she was comfortable with. But with Jamie, things were different. He'd urged her to come out of her shell, and, surprisingly, she'd agreed, confident that he would step up if it was too much for her. That alone must mean something, shouldn't it? "Anyway, Jamie shouldn't be as hard to please as…say, you or Rhys would be. If you could just do me this favor…" Horror overcame her. "I mean, you kissed me once. I know it didn't mean anything but…well, the idea…it doesn't, well, gross you out, does it?"

"What? Of course not." But he was looking panicked now. His hand moved to rub the back of his neck. "It's just, I don't want you thinking there's anything wrong with you. You're just, you're just—"

"An amateur?" she suggested.

"Well, I was going to say selective, but given the men you've chosen, you obviously haven't been picking from the cream of the crop."

"What's that supposed to mean?"

"Please. I've met the guys."

"They were all smart. Influential. Okay, so they're not tall and handsome and fly to London to perform for the queen, but—"

"They were pansies. And it sounds like this guy you want to bang is a pansy, too."

"He is not a pansy. And the others were just uninspired."

"Melina—"

She shook her head. "Tell me the truth. You go for experienced women. Women who know how to please you in bed."

"Well, sure, but—"

"In the insect world, bugs mate for one reason and one reason only, because they get something out of it. I want a mate, Max. I want to know how to keep one. So, if it doesn't disgust you to be with me, can you please do me this favor?"

He seemed to think about it. "Why me? Why not Rhys?"

Because I'm not safe with Rhys, she thought. *Not the way I am with you.* With Rhys, assuming that he would even agree to it, it wouldn't be about simple biology, learning positions and technique, or walking away when the session was over. With Rhys, she'd lose herself. She'd start believing in unicorns and flying dragons and mutual passion leading to lifelong happiness. She'd want more than she could have. "Why Rhys and not you?" she hedged.

"Come on, Melina. We both know that of the two of us, I'm the bastard. I'm the…the—"

"Man whore?"

He cleared his throat. "Again, I was going to say least discriminating."

"Be that as it may, you've never left me hanging just so you could get laid." She held up her hand. "I know you're always trying to make excuses for Rhys's behavior that night, but it was lame. And you were there for me, just like you've always been. If that's not enough reason, the fact that you have the most experience is another point in your favor, right?"

He looked at her oddly. "Quantity doesn't necessarily equate to quality. Believe me, Rhys knows what he's doing."

The image of Rhys doing anything to her made her nerves tingle in interesting places and had her thighs clenching together. "Look, are you going to do it?" *Do me,* she amended internally. "Or not?"

"I'll ask again. Why me?"

"Because I trust you."

"And?"

"Because you'll be nice. During. And afterward. At least, I thought you would. Now I'm not so sure," she said pointedly.

"Sex with me isn't nice, Melina. Sex done right isn't nice at all."

She swallowed hard. It had suddenly gotten hot in here. "So show me."

"What if I say no?"

"Then I'll find someone else."

"Rhys?"

"Argh! What is your obsession with your brother? Is this some kind of weird kinky twin thing? Do you want me to say his name when we're doing it?"

"No," he said, obviously struggling for patience. "I want you to tell me who you'll go to if I say no."

She shrugged.

"What's that mean? You'd just do it with some stranger?"

"Haven't you?"

Fascinated, she watched him turn red. "We're not talking about me. And you're talking about this as if it's one of your damn experiments. You can't just decide you want to be a sex diva and ask me to teach you how, Melina."

"Actually, we are talking about you. And that's exactly what I'm asking for."

3

Dalton's Magic Rule # 4:
Practice with the right tools.

Overnight bag with toiletries. Check.
Sexy underwear. Check.
Contraception. Check.
Hotel room.
Duh.

Melina stared at the three brass numbers affixed to Max's hotel room door. They hadn't changed in the five minutes she'd been standing there looking at them. She had the right room. She had everything she needed. Let the sex education begin.

Right?

Biting her lip, she closed her eyes and tried to talk herself into sticking the key card into the little slot. Inserting part A into part B had never been her problem. It's what happened afterward that she clearly lacked skill in.

Still, she hesitated.

Something about this felt wrong.

Could she really get naked with Max? Touch him? Let him touch her?

The image of him looming over her in bed, surrounding her with warm skin and hard muscles, certainly wasn't unappealing, but it wasn't exactly pulling her tractor either.

Maybe there really was something wrong with her.

"Face it, Melina," Brian had said to her after she'd found him in bed with one of his veterinary residents. "A man needs more than a stiff board underneath him when he wants to screw. Doesn't matter how well-cushioned it is. You show more passion for the bugs in your lab than you do me. Take my advice. Get some practice in before you try to nab a guy again."

She hadn't broken down at the accusation. In fact, she'd handled herself like the lady she was, even letting him take the dog they'd adopted from the pound a year before. Then she'd called Lucy and Grace, and the three of them had thrown darts at Brian's pictures while drinking sangria. Still, the knowledge that what she and Brian had been doing was "screwing" when she'd thought they'd been making love had haunted her for days.

And the worst part was, he'd been right. In previous relationships, she'd tried to be an active lover, only to score low when it came to evaluations. With Brian, she'd been content to let him take the lead, thinking that's what he wanted. Apparently, screwing was more complicated than she'd thought, and like it or not, she was going to get the practice that Brian had so cruelly suggested.

In scientific terms, it simply made sense.

Lady in public. Whore in the bedroom. She could do that, right?

Five minutes later, still standing in the same location, she thought, apparently not.

She leaned her forehead on the door and thumped it twice. The second time, not so gently.

What are you waiting for?

Max was gorgeous. Sexy. He cared about her. Plus, she'd sworn him to secrecy. Other than Lucy and Grace, who'd expect a full report, no one would know about this but the two of them. And if he couldn't bring out her inner slut, who could?

Rhys's name popped into her head.

Just like that, the image of her and Max morphed into her and Rhys. Of course, the picture didn't change all that much given they were twins, but her reaction to it did. It was as if it had been two-dimensional before but suddenly had turned real. She could feel the heat of Rhys's bare skin, see the sweat dotting his forehead, and hear his groans of pleasure as he moved against her. Inside her.

And lo and behold, she was even on top this time, normally not one of her favorite positions.

Closing her eyes, she valiantly ignored the sudden wetness between her legs.

Yep. How twisted was that? They looked identical, but only one of them got her hot. And it was the one who didn't even care enough about her to call.

Max cared, she reminded herself. And they were good enough friends that they could do this. She'd just look upon it as an experiment. Two days of trial runs and data analysis. Then Max would get back on a plane to Vegas or wherever his next show was, and the next time they saw each other, she'd be happy and in love with Jamie. Maybe she'd even be pregnant if the next Dalton Twins' Magic Show tour went on for a while.

The image of her holding a baby cinched it. She stuck the card in the slot, waited for the green light, and pushed the door open.

* * *

In the lobby bar, Rhys watched Max check his watch for about the tenth time. His brother was acting weird, no two ways about it. Leaning back in his chair, he raised his hand and wiggled his fingers. "Spill it."

"Huh?"

"What's going on? You've been acting like a nervous Nellie since I got here. What did Melina say that you couldn't tell me on the phone?"

Max's brow quirked. "Nervous Nellie?"

"You know what I mean, butthead. Now what the hell's going on?"

"Butthead? Your skill with words is mind-boggling." At Rhys's low growl, Max held up his hands. "All right already. Will you just ease up? I already told you it wasn't an emergency."

Rhys barely refrained from grabbing his brother by the throat. "Your exact message was: 'Something weird is going on with Melina. Get your ass on a plane right now.' You refused to answer any of my calls, so that's exactly what I did."

"Would you have gotten on the plane if I'd said I needed your advice about something?"

Rhys slammed his palms on the table. "Damn it, Max, I don't have time for this. You have ten seconds to start talking or I'm driving back to the airport."

"It's her birthday."

Stunned, Rhys stared at him for several seconds before answering. "Yeah, I know. That's why I told you to tell her happy birthday." It was also why he'd thrown her present in his suitcase during his frantic rush to get a flight. Just in case.

Max lifted his drink—water instead of his usual beer—and took a healthy swallow. Rhys narrowed his eyes. What was going on here?

"All that stuff you said about her wanting the white picket fence and two-point-two kids? That stuff doesn't matter," Max said softly. "You're hurting her."

The accusation caught him off guard, but he couldn't deny it either. He looked away.

"She's not an idiot, Rhys. She recognizes that you've pulled away. That you don't call. You don't visit. Hell, she's certain you forgot about her birthday. And why wouldn't she? You two barely say anything to each other anymore."

Rhys gritted his teeth. "She works with her bugs. Visits her parents once a month. Dates safe, nice guys. What else is there to know?"

"How about what that so-called ex-boyfriend of hers did to her?"

Rhys sat straight up. Was that what Max's call had been about? What had been the loser's name? Bradley? Brian? Yeah, Brian. Had he hurt her? Hit her? A slow but intense wash of anger began to pump in his veins. "What?"

Max shook his head in disgust. "Nothing. Forget I said anything."

Rhys stood, braced his hands on the table, and got nose to nose with his brother. "I'm not forgetting anything. Tell me. Did he hurt her?"

Max leaned back and spread out his hands in a welcoming gesture. "And what if he did? What are you going to do about it? Scare him to death so he pisses his pants like Scott Thompson did?"

"I'll kill him," Rhys spit out from between his teeth.

Max stared at him, then grinned. "I believe you would."

"What are you grinning at? I'd think you'd be right in line with me."

"I know I would. I'm just surprised you said it out loud. Where Melina is concerned, you're prone to changing the subject."

Straightening, Rhys raked his hands through his hair.

"Since when has there been any question that I care about Melina? She's one of the sweetest..." Sexiest. Hottest. Most intriguing. "...women I know, and we've known her for years. Hell, Mom and Dad would get in line to beat the guy up, too."

"Then why? If you care so much about her, why don't you finally lay it on the table?"

Rhys shook his finger. "Oh no. We're not having that conversation again. Stop playing games, Max. I just want to know if Melina's okay and whether I'm going to have to kill anyone tonight."

Max shrugged. "She's okay. Her boyfriend bruised her pride, that's all. She's more hurt by your callous actions than anything else. I know you didn't want to come here, but I'm not apologizing. You can damn well say happy birthday to her face."

Rhys practically fell into his chair. He wanted to rail at his brother for his deceptive tactics, but his own guilt weighed on him heavily. He hadn't thought that his pulling away would hurt Melina that much. Then again, he hadn't thought beyond wanting to stop his pain. But Max was right. Melina was his friend. It wasn't her fault he wanted her to be more. "First thing in the morning, I promise."

"Good. You still going to fly to Reno?"

"Right after I see her."

"We don't have to be in Reno for another few days. You're obsessing—"

"The last time we worked the Magic Underground,

the backstage crew was a disaster. And you weren't the one caught trying to do an Omni Deck in front of five hundred people only to flounder when it didn't happen. I'm not going to let something like that happen when the Seven Seas contract is at stake."

His brother reached out and placed his hand on Rhys's arm. "You've always been the brains behind our success, Rhys. I know that, and so do Mom and Dad. No one can take that success away from us, even if we don't end up getting Seven Seas."

A little stunned by Max's admission, Rhys said, "We'll get the contract so long as everything goes as planned."

Max gave a curt nod, then stood. Rhys looked at him in surprise. "Where are you headed?"

"There's a blonde at the bar who's eyeballing us. Unless you've changed your prudish ways and want to join us—"

Rhys didn't even bother looking at the woman. "Go ahead. I'm going to turn in. I'm beat."

"Yeah. You really should turn in." Max turned, paused, then turned back. "It's been a hell of a decade on the road, don't you think?"

"It's been fun. The best."

Max nodded, then grinned. "Get all the rest you can, you hear? I'll see you not-so-bright-and-early Monday morning at the Magic Underground."

Rhys watched his brother approach the blonde, who looked at Rhys and waved. Rhys smiled and waved back, his public persona firmly in place, but he swiftly turned away.

He dismissed the idea of having another beer. He hadn't been exaggerating when he said he was tired. He'd had to catch two layovers to fly from Kentucky to Sacramento. Of course, being that it was last-minute, the flight had cost a small fortune. In the end, it hadn't mattered.

Even before Max had called, Rhys had been getting ready to book a flight. Max's call had just added some panic to the long trip. He couldn't let Melina think he'd forgotten her birthday. As much as it would solidify the distance he'd been gradually establishing between them, he couldn't hurt her that way. Instinctively, he knew it would be a hurt he couldn't repair, and the thought of making that final break had been terrifying.

As had been his sudden, inexplicable certainty that she needed him.

Maybe it was some kind of twin telepathy or something.

Melina had clearly confided her relationship troubles to Max and sworn him to secrecy. The idea of either Melina or Max keeping secrets from him was unsettling but not surprising. Why would she confide in him when he'd been doing his best to push her way?

More disturbing was the idea that her ex had hurt her.

Possessiveness swamped him, but he easily pushed it down. He'd had so much practice at it, after all. Melina wasn't his, but she was still someone extremely special to him. If someone had hurt her, even if it was just her pride, he'd pay for it. Rhys would make sure of that.

"Excuse me?"

Rhys glanced up at the soft, feminine voice. It was the blonde from the bar. Frowning, he glanced over his shoulder but saw no sign of Max.

"Your brother was telling me about your act. He's going to get his car. I was wondering if you'd mind company. My friend Jocelyn over there," she pointed to a rail-thin brunette who was sitting at the bar and watching them, "is a doll, and I'd feel horrible abandoning her."

But she'd still do it, Rhys thought, trying not to judge his brother's taste in women. He'd made plenty of bad decisions in his life, so he had no business judging anyone. Shaking his head, he began to rise. "I'm sorry, but I was just about to—"

"Hi." The brunette strode up to his table and held out her hand. "I am so thrilled to meet you. I absolutely love your magic act. Would you mind if I join you?"

Sighing, Rhys sat back in his chair and watched as the blonde backed away, waved, and bee-lined for the exit, presumably to meet his brother. He focused on the brunette. She was decked out, fit, and had a charming smile, but he just wanted to go up to bed. Alone. The last thing he wanted was to talk about magic right now. But he didn't want to be rude to a fan either. "So where did you see the act?" he asked, catching the eye of the waiter and indicating he wanted another beer.

* * *

As Melina entered the hotel room, she half-expected Max to have done it up. Candles. Flowers. Something. But it was in its normal state, the linens straightened and the towels in the bathroom folded neatly, indicating that housekeeping had come and gone. Melina let out a sigh of relief.

Max was sticking to the plan, making this weekend exactly what she wanted, a straightforward tutoring session rather than something resembling a romantic rendezvous or false seduction. When a woman asked you to teach her how to please a man, very little seduction was necessary, after all. Pretending otherwise would have made her feel even more self-conscious.

Setting her single bag on the bed, she noted that Max had traveled pretty light himself. A suitcase in the corner, along with the familiar-looking magic case that held his cards and smaller close-up tricks. An evil urge to open the case and rifle through it took hold of her, but of course she couldn't do it. A magician's bag of tricks was his sacred possession. Neither Max nor Rhys had ever broken the magician's code by telling her how a trick was performed.

Of course, she'd done her own research on the Internet, but had never told them that. They would have been appalled. Growing up with professional magicians as parents had made Max and Rhys not just passionate about the craft, but mystical in many ways. They talked as if they actually believed it was possible to make a card appear from thin air. And they wanted her to have such belief as well.

Lucky for her, her scientific mind couldn't subscribe to such fodder. It was always better to deal with concretes. That way, you could calculate the risks and predict the outcome. Even then, the world was a scary place. Add something like magic to the equation? No, thanks.

It didn't take her very long to unpack, and soon she found herself sitting on the edge of the bed, trying to stop herself from bolting.

Chewing on one nail, she glanced at the hotel clock. 7:30 p.m. Max had told her he would be back to the hotel room close to 8:30 p.m. and to get comfortable and wait for him.

"And by comfortable, I don't mean sweats and a ratty T-shirt, Melina. Bring something sexy to wear," he'd ordered. "Wear your hair down. And ditch the glasses."

"But I can't see well without my glasses," she'd protested. "I mean, I won't run into walls, but I'll miss the finer details."

Something like satisfaction sparked in his eyes, but then his expression went blank. "Don't you have contacts?"

"I can't wear contacts. I have dry eyes."

Shaking his head with amusement, he said, "Just do it, babe." Then he'd leaned forward, kissed her forehead as he'd done so many times in the past, and got up to leave. Before closing the door, however, he'd turned back to her. "You sure about this?"

Of course she wasn't sure, she'd wanted to scream.

But he'd already said yes. Plus, she didn't relish the idea of telling fifty undergraduate students that she was a sexual coward. And, finally, she'd forced herself to remember the shame she'd felt at Brian's words. Telling her she wasn't good enough, sexy enough, to inspire a man's passion. She was never going to let another man hurt her that way again, and she trusted Max to teach her things that would put Brian's little vet resident to shame.

"I'm sure," she'd said. "After all, tomorrow's my birthday. What could be better for me than a little continuing education?"

Education? What a dork, she'd thought. Thankfully, he'd just smiled. "That's right. Remember, no glasses, okay?"

"Are they really that ugly?" she'd asked hesitantly, lifting one hand to touch the wire frames she'd once thought were quite stylish.

All he'd done was close the door, loudly singing *Happy Birthday to You*, as he walked down the walkway to his car.

She'd felt so self-satisfied then. Giddy that he'd agreed to help her. Now, she stared at the single large piece of luggage that had been laid across the luggage rack as if it contained something horrible. Standing, she walked toward it, stopping when she saw a few items that Max had laid on the long surface of the dresser. A black toiletry bag. A bottle of cologne. A comb. And—

Her eyes widened, and she reached out, nudging the cologne bottle aside. There, sticking half-out of a toiletry bag, was a box of condoms. Hand shaking, she picked it up.

It was open. Looking around as if to make sure no one had snuck into the room while she'd been distracted, she read the label more closely. Good thing he'd come prepared because what she'd bought wasn't nearly as interesting. She'd gone for the standard stuff, whereas his tastes ran to Magnum extra large, ribbed, and flavored. She flushed but couldn't resist grabbing one of the foil-wrapped Magnums and studying it.

The men she'd been with had all been of like size, and she knew they'd fit well within the range of average. This condom didn't look unusually big. Really, how much difference was there between Magnum and acceptable? Was it just a marketing device designed to play on a man's insecurities? There was one sure way to tell.

Rifling through her own bag, she took out one of the condoms she'd brought. Sitting cross-legged on the bed, she ripped open each foil packet and laid the small latex disks on the coverlet. Dragging her purse closer to her, she extracted the small measuring tape in one of the side pockets. Pursing her lips, she unrolled both condoms then laid them flat.

After some quick measurements, she sat back.

Okay, there was a definite difference. She couldn't accuse the condom makers of false advertisement. The Magnums were indeed about thirty percent larger than the regular-size condoms. Mostly in width, since the condom wasn't designed to fit the entire length of a man's penis anyway.

Feeling light-headed, she tried to envision herself helping Max put one of those things on.

All that did was make her start hyperventilating.

Stop it, she told herself. *Don't go there.*

To distract herself, Melina carefully tucked both unused rubbers into her overnight bag. She couldn't very well leave them in the trash can and risk Max seeing them and guessing what she'd done. He'd tease her about it mercilessly.

He'd probably tease her about this whole situation once the shock wore off.

If he showed up in the first place.

Breath catching, she once again felt dizzy. Frantic.

Desperately, she searched the room, her gaze landing on the minibar. She rushed to it, opened the door, and stared at the little bottles of alcohol.

She'd seen a stocked minibar before, but she'd never actually drank from it. Too expensive. Plus, the little bottles of alcohol had seemed silly somehow. Right now, silly seemed appropriate, and she was desperate to calm her jittery nerves. Taking out the five small bottles, she lined them up on top of the dresser and perused the selection. One finger tapping her pursed lips, she selected one bottle. Unscrewing the cap, she took a swig.

And gasped.

Holy moly, that burned.

The second swig, not so much.

By the time she took her third, she was already

starting to feel better.

She set the bottle down then looked at the clock. It was almost eight.

Max would be here soon, and she was still fully dressed, hardly what one would call comfortably.

Rushing into the bathroom, she stripped down to her underwear, simple boy-short panties and a cotton camisole and bra. Face flushed with nerves and alcohol, she stared at herself in the full-length mirror.

What she'd told Max was true. She wasn't beautiful, and she didn't have the world's best body, but she was attractive. Certainly nothing like he and Rhys were used to, but Max must find her at least reasonably attractive, or else he wouldn't have agreed to her little proposal.

Unless he felt sorry for her.

Oh, God. Was she about to be pity fucked?

The idea didn't sit well with her. She was a strong, independent woman who simply wanted to expand her repertoire of tricks. She'd read sex books. She'd watched porn. But besides making her incredibly hot and frustrated, most of the sexual acts and responses she'd viewed still seemed somewhat perplexing to her. The whole thing with the nipples, for example. Nipple stimulation did next to nothing for her, but other women seemed to enjoy it. Did men?

That was the kind of thing she wanted to know. The kind of thing that Brian had ridiculed her for when she'd asked him. She'd ply Max with questions, and she'd try her best to make the experience a good one for him.

It wasn't like he could have very many expectations.

At least she knew she was a better kisser than she'd been at sixteen.

Closing her eyes, she opened herself to the memory of that long-ago night. Rhys had asked her to meet him in her parents' gazebo the night of her sweet sixteen party. He had something special he wanted to give her, he'd said. And something important to tell her. Imagination going wild and hope soaring, she'd waited in that gazebo for over an hour before Max had come out to find her. When she'd asked about Rhys, Max had stalled. But Melina had kept pushing until Max finally admitted that Rhys was making out with Trisha James, the busty blonde cheerleader who lived next door and the one who Melina's parents had bullied her into inviting. She'd sobbed all over poor Max's shirt, and then, feeling sorry for her, he'd kissed her. Even then, she hadn't been ignorant of his skill. That slow, gentle, open-mouthed kiss still ranked high on her kiss-o-meter. By the time Rhys had shown up outside, Trisha by his side, Melina had been able to control her hurt and make a dignified exit.

She'd always been grateful to Max for his compassion that night. That's why she knew he wouldn't let her down now.

Another quick glance at the clock confirmed she had about twenty more minutes until he showed up.

She climbed on the bed. She tried out several come-hither positions, but only felt exposed and silly. Finally, she settled for getting under the covers, but not before putting the minibar bottles on the end table next to her, lined up like little shot glasses.

Just a little more whiskey courage, she thought.

She was on the last bottle, an enjoyable buzz simmering inside her, when she remembered Max's third request.

Her glasses. She took them off, stared blurrily at the fragile frames, and moved to put them on the nightstand. She hesitated. With a shrug, she tossed the glasses in the direction of the armchair, wincing when she heard them bounce against something hard.

No matter. She had a spare pair in her purse and more at home.

Tonight was supposed to be all about experiencing new things.

New sensations.

She was going to be a good little pupil.

She knew, however, that, like a shot in the arm that was for her own good, sometimes it was better to not see what was coming. Especially if it was of magnum proportions.

* * *

Rhys got off the elevator and moved wearily toward his hotel room. He was standing in front of his door and fishing his key card from his pocket when he suddenly froze. Head tilted back, he took a deep breath. He smelled lemon, a fresh, clean scent that he always associated with

Melina because of the shampoo her mother had customized for her long, curly, brown locks. His gut clenched as he replayed his conversation with Max.

His brother had landed two blows over the course of two days. The first, by exposing his feelings for Melina. The second, by accusing him of hurting her. Both right on the mark.

He didn't want to hurt Melina. That's the last thing he wanted. But after over a decade of having what he wanted just within his reach but knowing he couldn't have it, he needed to move on.

Hell, he and Max were celebrities. Women threw themselves at him. The brunette he'd left at the bar had made it clear she was interested in more than his autograph and had seemed genuinely disappointed when he'd wished her goodnight.

Still, while one or two had managed to catch his attention for more than a night over the years, they'd never been able to make him feel the way he felt when he was with Melina.

As though a part of him had long been chopped off and magically reattached.

Like a deck of cards missing all its aces until someone slipped them back in.

It was a feeling that even the thundering applause of a packed theater in Caesars Palace couldn't compete with.

But it was an illusion. She'd already shown she preferred Max's company by a wide mile. Plus, beyond physical attraction on his part and possibly on hers, they weren't compatible, and he didn't want to spend his life arguing with her or disappointing her just to be proved right.

Shaking his head, he slipped the key card in and entered the hotel room.

Immediately, he tensed, his sharp vision homing in on the woman lying in his bed, her eyes sleepily blinking open as she propped herself up on one elbow. He almost swallowed his tongue when the sheet slipped down her chest, exposing her graceful throat and bare shoulders and arms. Her hair, usually pulled back, tumbled around her face like a cloud of mink.

Like a man under a spell, he walked into the room. Stumbled was probably more like it. He heard the loud click of the door closing behind him.

She smiled. "Hi."

He trembled at the simple word, spoken in a husky, sleepy tone he'd never heard come from her lips. His hands clenched into fists as an inferno ignited inside him, spreading from his groin into his extremities. His dick filled with blood, hardening so fast that he would have grimaced with the pleasure-pain if he was capable of it.

Instead, he stared at her and struggled to speak.

She scooted to a sitting position and tucked the sheet around her. "I-I must have dozed off." She glanced at the clock, squinting a bit without her glasses.

When had he last seen her without her glasses?

"Everything okay?" she asked.

His soggy brain struggled to work. Okay? Things

were looking fucking fabulous from where he was standing.

"So, did you want to clean up first or—" She cleared her throat. "Or just get started?"

His mouth dropped open. Worked up and down. "Started," he finally managed to croak. He'd intended the word to be a question, but it came out as a definitive statement.

She shot him another sweet smile, and he instinctively stepped closer. God, she looked amazing. And the way she was staring at him, so warm and at ease, a look she hadn't given him in such a long time. It made his chest ache. It made his heart pound.

It made his dick throb even more.

She held out a hand. "Then come here, big boy, and teach me what you like."

4

Dalton's Magic Rule #5:
Get up close and personal.

Part of Melina knew she should be freaking out. She couldn't quite comprehend why she wasn't. Somewhere between getting into bed and Max's arrival, a veil of calm certainty had surrounded her. She felt like Super Sex Goddess Woman. Like she could do anything. Do anyone. Especially now that she'd done herself.

The words echoed in her mind, and she almost giggled. Although she suppressed the urge, she couldn't stop the way her legs shifted guiltily beneath the blankets.

Could Max tell what she'd been up to before he'd walked in? Thank God, the tremors of her self-induced orgasm had already dwindled. And it certainly wasn't a crime. In fact, it had made perfect sense to her as she'd lain staring at the ceiling, her nerves eased but her mind still working a hundred miles a minute.

Max was her friend, true, but there was no doubt that

he was also overwhelmingly hot and way out of her league. Despite Brian's comments to the contrary, she got as horny as the next woman. Maybe even more so, for all she knew. That wouldn't serve her well tonight. If she was all aroused and stimulated when Max climbed into bed with her, she wouldn't be able to concentrate on the task at hand. Since she had always been a one-a-day girl if she was lucky, it made sense that giving herself an orgasm would help her remain sufficiently clearheaded throughout the evening.

Satisfied with her reasoning, she'd slid her hand inside her underwear and taken care of business, rubbing and pressing and dipping in ways she thought were quite simple but Brian hadn't been able to get a basic handle on. When she'd felt her pleasure building, she'd closed her eyes and given into one of her favorite fantasies.

It involved her and Rhys. And water. Lots of water. Rain pounding down on them, plastering their clothes to their bodies. Rhys tossing her skirt up and pressing her up against a porch post while she wrapped her legs around his waist. But the rain on the outside would be nothing compared to the warm wetness that would help ease his way inside her. His cock would be thick and long. Rock hard. Big and beautiful and filling her to perfection so that she'd go crazy in his arms—right before he went crazy in hers.

Imagining his hips thrusting and bucking while he shouted her name to the heavens had made her body clench with delight. The pressure inside her had mounted, spinning out of control until it had finally snapped. She'd bitten her lip as she'd savored one pulse of pleasure after another. Of course, as the sensations had ebbed, and she'd found herself dry and alone in her bed, she'd bitten her lip again—this time in an effort to stifle her moan of pain.

She'd ached inside when she'd realized it had just been another fantasy. Just like she always ached for Rhys. And just when she'd started to fall asleep, with the vague idea that maybe Max wasn't going to show, she'd heard the hotel door open.

Now here he was, standing no more than five feet from the bed, his tall form as broad-shouldered and powerful as the one she'd conjured in her fantasy. And although she was a little nervous because she didn't know exactly what was going to happen, she wasn't freaking out. In fact, that slow, lazy glide of slick pleasure had started inside her again, weighing her down with a pleasant but confusing infusion of desire. Obviously, her eyes were seeing Max, but her body was ready to reach out and touch Rhys.

Even without her glasses, she could tell Max was feeling a little off-kilter, as well. Somehow, that gave her added courage.

Wow. She was about to get her game on with one of the Dalton twins, maybe not the right one, but at least the one who, unlike most men in her life, was here to give her what she needed and not the other way around.

Well, kinda.

She took a deep breath. It's showtime.

Swinging her feet over the side of the bed, she got to her feet, then immediately threw out a steadying hand when she swayed.

Whoa. Not wearing her glasses was not only putting a hazy edge to her vision, but throwing her equilibrium off balance, too. Shaking back her hair, her hand still gliding over the bedcovers for balance, she skirted around the mattress toward Max. Deliberately, she threw her shoulders back and kept her chin up.

She was tired of men who sucked in bed and blamed her for their suckiness. She'd take her fair share of responsibility, but not all of it. At least she was proactive. At least she was willing to learn. And who knew? She was a good student. If Max was a good enough teacher, maybe she could make her fantasy come true. Not with Rhys, of course, but maybe with Jamie. And if not with him, then maybe someone else.

Coming to an abrupt halt, she smiled. She was starting to think that her vow to give herself one last chance to find a man was silly. She'd never been a quitter, after all. Pleased with her realization, she raised her gaze to Max.

He hadn't moved. Just continued to stare at her as if her offer to please him had rendered him speechless or, at the very least, given him second thoughts.

They couldn't have that.

Raising her arms, she turned in a slow circle, ending the show with her hands resting on her hips. "Well? Is this sexy enough for you?"

* * *

Sexy enough?

Was she sexy enough for him?

Rhys licked his lips, but was careful not to make any sudden moves. If he was losing his marbles, he wasn't about to do anything to rattle his brain back to life. With her simple camisole and boy-short underwear, she was showing less skin than women often showed at the pool. Hell, the girls wore less material on stage.

But this was Melina, and he was seeing parts of her he'd never seen before. The surprisingly deep shadow of her cleavage that looked velvety smooth. Hard-tipped nipples poking against the double layer of her bra and thin camisole. And the buttery, smooth skin of her upper thighs that pressed together just underneath the vee of her pussy. Groaning, he couldn't decide which crevice he wanted to explore with his tongue first. The one between her breasts or the one that was trying to protect the vulnerable folds of her sex along with her simple yet feminine underwear.

"Are you okay?"

His gaze jumped to hers. A small furrow had formed between her brows. As he watched, her already pink cheeks flushed until they were cherry red. He saw the moment insecurity began to replace her bravado.

That jerked him out of his daze fast.

She was offering him what he'd craved for years. He

wasn't about to embarrass her.

Moving the last few steps toward her, he raised his hand, stroked her hair from her face, then cupped the back of her neck. With his other hand, he tilted her chin up. "I'm good. Better than good. I just never thought you'd actually do it. Come to me, I mean."

"Of course I would, silly. I have nothing to do all weekend but learn what pleases you. It's my birthday present to myself."

Rhys's chest tightened. He was her birthday present? Since when? Was it because he hadn't called her? That he'd tried his best to drive her away? Had maintaining his distance finally made Melina realize how much she wanted him? If so, the agony had been worth it. "You've got it wrong, sweetheart. You're giving me the present, and it's not my birthday for another six months."

But what about his reasons for staying away from her, his inner, and wholly annoying, voice interrupted. The picket fence? The two-point-two kids?

He slapped the voice away fast. He wasn't thinking about that. He couldn't. Not with Melina in front of him.

"Do you want to—" She raised a hand and pressed it against his shirt. "You know. Undress?"

"Is that what you want?" When she nodded her head, he moved to step back, but then froze. He couldn't let go of her yet. He kneaded her neck, loving the way her eyes glazed over and she bit her lip with strong, white teeth. "Do you want to know what I want?"

She cleared her throat. "Of course. That's why I'm

here, remember?"

Right. She was here because, by some miracle, she wanted to know what turned him on. As with magic and most other things, action was his favorite means of communication.

He bent down, and her eyes narrowed in that adorable semi-squint again. When his closed lips touched hers, they fluttered shut completely. Thinking she had the right idea, he closed his eyes and savored that first moment of contact.

It was like diving into heaven. Her lips were soft. Her breath even softer. Gently at first, his tongue sought hers. Rubbed. Parried. Thrust. When her breath hitched, he growled and opened his mouth wider, angling his head for optimum penetration.

Her mouth was so sweet, her taste so intoxicating, that he immediately imagined how sweet she'd taste in other places. Beneath his pants, his cock swelled to such stiff readiness that his ragged groan sounded tortured. Shakily, he pulled away. "I need more of you. Need to feel you against me."

Her eyes were fixed on his fingers as he unbuttoned his shirt, but when he finished the last button, he reached for her. "Let's get you comfortable first," he said. To his surprise, she shook her head.

Instead of backing away from him, however, she moved closer, snaked her hands inside his open shirt, and placed her palms against his chest. With a look of wonder, she slid her hands up, then down, then up again. "You're so—" She swallowed audibly. "You're so warm and hard."

He wasn't just warm. He was hot, and her hands on his bare skin were burning him alive. "Melina," he groaned. Wrapping his fingers around her wrist, he dragged her hand down to his throbbing dick. "Here. Just for a minute," he pleaded. "Please touch me here."

He let go of her hand, but she didn't move, and he wondered if he'd moved too fast too soon. But then she cupped him through his jeans and rubbed gently. His head fell back, and he gritted his teeth at the pleasure.

"Does that feel good?"

He glanced down, but she wasn't looking at him. At least not at his face. Her gaze was plastered to her hand and what it was doing to him. "It feels like heaven," he gasped out. "Better than heaven."

That made her look at him. "What could be better than heaven?" she teased from beneath heavy eyelids.

He couldn't resist touching her any longer. He cupped her breasts, pushing them together and deepening her cleavage before he buried his face in it. Kneading her breasts gently, he dipped his tongue inside her top and into her soft skin. "So sweet." Slowly, one hand dropped down to the hot spot between her thighs, making her jerk. "So hot. Are you wet, Melina?"

"I-I—"

He raised his head to look at her. "Are you?" he crooned.

She just shook her head.

"No?"

She shook her head again. "I-I—"

"It's okay," he said. "How about I find out for myself?"

He curled his fingers around and underneath one leg of her underwear. He groaned when her juices immediately covered his fingertips. She whimpered. "Oh, yeah. You're wet. Just like I've always imagined." He found the hard nub of her clitoris and pressed firmly against it.

"Oh, my God," she panted. "What are you doing? I'm supposed to be pleasing you."

He chuckled. "Believe me. Nothing pleases me more than knowing that you're wet and hungry for me. You hungry, Melina?"

Slowly, he pushed one finger inside her. The hand cupping his dick tightened then dropped away completely, moving to grab his wrist. She didn't try to pull his hand away, just held him in a tight grip as if she wasn't sure what she should do.

Good thing he knew exactly what he was going to do.

A second finger joined the first, and he twisted them, curving them to find the spot that made her head drop onto his shoulder and her moans louder. She was trembling hard, but he suddenly realized that he was, too.

Abruptly, his patience left him and his need grabbed him by the throat like a wolf going in for the kill. "You know what else I like, Ladybug? A big, soft bed underneath me when I make love." When he tried to withdraw his fingers from her, her grip on his wrist suddenly tightened and tried to keep him where he was. He bent down and kissed her, using his teeth this time to add a new dimension to her pleasure. Slipping his wrist from her hold, he swung her up in his arms, carried her to the bed, and gently tossed her down. "Undress. Now."

He saw her eyes widen at the hoarse command, but he was already frantically ripping off his shirt even as he kicked off his shoes. He unbuttoned his jeans and shoved them down his hips, underwear and all, and left them on the floor with his socks. When he looked up, she hadn't moved. She was staring at his dick, a look of amazement on her face that made him swell even more.

"You're definitely magnum-sized," she whispered.

He hardly registered the comment. He was a little bigger than average, but she'd have no trouble taking him. Grabbing her ankles, he pulled her toward him and reached for the bottom of her camisole.

"Wait—" she squeaked.

He pulled her top over her head and threw it across the room. Eyes taking in her lacy bra and the plump flesh filling it, he reached for her shorts.

"I want to see you. I want to touch you," she insisted.

The shorts followed the camisole. Just as she had stared at him, he couldn't take his eyes off of her pussy. Holy crap, he thought. *Who would have thought it?*

"You've got a Brazilian," he choked out as he reached out to caress the tiny strip of chocolate-brown curls.

She cleared her throat. "Actually, the girl who did it

told me it's called a Metro Strip. She told me to go for a heart, but that seemed a little too silly given what we're—"

"Did you get this for tonight?"

She hesitated, then nodded her head.

He ran a finger through her pink, sweet flesh, parting her until his mouth watered. Pushing his finger inside her then slowly easing it out, he watched it grow more and more damp as he pumped it gently inside her. Her muscles clenched him, trying to hang on, sucking him so tight that sweat beaded on his forehead.

He dropped to his knees, shouldered his way between her thighs, and prepared to eat his fill of her. Quick as lightning, she reached out to cover herself, something that was hard to do with his finger still inside her, and he growled in frustration.

"This is supposed to be about your pleasure," she reminded him.

That did it. Extracting his finger, he raised himself up, stared right at her, and licked her juice off his finger. When her eyes widened, he grabbed both her wrists, stretched her arms above her head, and leaned down until they were nose to nose. "You want to please me?" he breathed.

She nodded her head.

"Then this is what you're going to do." He leaned down and kissed her neck, trailed a string of kisses to her ear, and then nipped at her earlobe before swiping it slowly with his tongue. "You're going to use your hands for one thing and one thing only. You're going to unhook your bra and bare your breasts. Then you're going to cup them. Your fingers are free to do whatever you want there. Tease your nipples. Pinch them tightly or gently. You do whatever turns you on. But you are not going to cover yourself from me. You're going to let me touch you and lick you and do whatever the hell I damn well please to please you, do you understand?"

"Is that...is that what you really want or are you just being nice?"

Laughing, he gentled his hold on her wrists and guided them to her breasts and the front clasp of her bra. "I want that more than anything in the world, Melina. I promise you."

She stared at him, her hesitation apparent. Then she nodded and twisted the clasp of her bra so that her small breasts spilled free.

* * *

Had she actually thought her breasts weren't sensitive?

Even with her blurry eyesight, she could see him looking at them. Granted, she couldn't tell whether his gaze was complimentary or not, but with his erection still pressed strong and sure against her belly, she'd place bets on it being complimentary. At least her breasts were convinced of that. They were swollen and achy—the type of achy that was indefinable yet intolerable to ignore.

Instinctively, she raised her hands and cupped herself, smoothing her palms from her rib cage to the rise of her breasts, her breath catching as the light pressure caused her nipples to tighten even more. Closing her eyes, she moaned. She pinched her nipples. Moaned even harder.

"That feel good, baby?"

Her only warning was the puff of breath against her skin before a warm, moist suction covered one nipple. With both nipples still pinched between her fingers, he alternatively flicked one and then the other with his tongue, making sure to give particular attention to the sensitive skin between her thumb and forefinger. Unable to help herself, she grabbed his hair and pressed him closer to her. "Please," she cried out brokenly.

"Please me?" he asked, a teasing lilt in his voice even as he replaced her fingers with his own, tweaking her nipples a tad bit harder than she had.

The corresponding tug in her sex had her arching off the bed. Shaking her head frantically, she said, "No, no. Please me. Suck me. Please."

"And then?"

"Then?" she echoed, her brain freezing.

"And then are you going to let me suck you all over?"

Her breath caught. So he hadn't lost sight of his original goal. As much as she was enjoying this, could she really handle him going down on her? She couldn't even think about that right now without getting a little dizzy. "Yes. Now please..." She lifted herself up, offering her breasts to him.

With a growl, he took what she'd offered, taking one nipple into his mouth and drawing on it strongly. With a pop, he released it, only to move on to the next one.

No, definitely not insensitive.

Her breasts were super sensitive, in fact.

So, so sensitive.

She almost cried out in loss when he raised his head, but he grasped her hands and placed them on her breasts again. "Now, keep your hands to yourself," he whispered.

She couldn't help it. She giggled.

He seemed to freeze. Seconds ticked by, and she shifted restlessly. "What?"

"I just...I just haven't heard you giggle in a while. I've missed it."

She tried to think back. Hadn't she giggled yesterday when they'd talked?

Who cared?

Who cared about anything but what he was going to do next. For a moment, she felt guilty at her thoughts. She'd never thought she'd have this wild, uncontrollable response to being touched by Max, and she was supposed to be concerned with his pleasure, not her own. But the more he touched her, the more he looked at her—

She jumped when his hands cupped her face and he leaned down toward her. "My pleasure, remember, Melina? You're not going to think about whatever you're thinking about because I already told you what you're going to do, right?"

"But—"

He kissed her hard, with an edge of domination that made her tremble. "Right?" he pressed.

"Right."

"And what are you going to do?" As if to remind her, he moved his hands to cover her own, guiding them to start a slow, erotic massage of her breasts.

"Touch myself."

"And what are you going to let me do to you?"

"Touch me?" she whispered.

"Be more specific."

"I-I—" Flushing in mortification, she shook her head. "Why don't you just do it instead?"

She heard his smile more than she saw it. "Don't you know that anticipation is half the pleasure? Do you know how long I've wanted to turn you on? I want to see it. Feel it. Hear it. So anticipate what I'm going to do to you, Melina. Tell me."

Licking her lips, she gathered her courage. "You're going to…kiss me. Lick me."

"Where? Here?" His hand stroked down her sternum to her navel and rubbed soft, lazy circles on her belly. Soon, he scooted his body down and his lips as well, planting tiny, sucking kisses down her body that made her writhe. "Or here?" Hands, then mouth, continued their descent before pausing just above her liquid core. Lifting his head and locking gazes with her, he stiffened his tongue and probed at the tender flesh until he homed in on the small nub that had swelled for his touch. "Or here?"

Before she could even try to respond, he licked lower, sweeping his tongue through her drenched folds until she could barely hold back her moans of pleasure.

Automatically, she raised one hand to cover her mouth. He lifted his head.

"Back on your breasts, Melina. I want to hear you scream, remember?"

She shook her head as reality suddenly crashed down on her. Desire could only sweep her away so far. She just wasn't the screaming type. "I don't scream," she said in a matter-of-fact voice that seemed completely at odds with the riotous emotions inside her.

"Never?"

"Never."

"Well, Ladybug. Looks like we're about to give ourselves the best present yet."

A vague ripple of confusion tugged at her brain, but it disappeared when he lowered his head, burying his face against her. He showed no hesitancy at all, but rather dove into her like a man starving for sustenance. He kissed and suckled and scraped his teeth lightly against her. He pierced her with his stiff tongue, then lapped at her clit with a moist, tender devotion that made her arch to get away, then arch for more. Using just his mouth at first, then adding his fingers to the mix, he plucked her like an instrument, occasionally humming and whispering to her—words of longing and sex and worship—until the sensations grew and grew and she had no choice but to do as he wanted.

She screamed as a tidal wave of pleasure slammed into her, only to be amazed when he started all over again.

She screamed as the second orgasm brought tears of

wonder to her eyes.

And she screamed as she struggled and strained and fought the pleasure he was determined to give her once more, crying that she couldn't take any more, that he was going to kill her, that no one had ever made her feel this way.

But he gave her no quarter. He worked her body as if she was a deck of cards, something plain and boring and static until he got his hands on it and worked his magic. When he was done, when he gave her a moment to breathe and cradled her in his arms, kissing the tears from her face and stroking her hair, she closed her eyes.

Almost instantly, with her head resting against his chest and his strong heartbeat beating in time to her own, she slipped into the fantasy. She could feel the warm rain beating down on her. The drag of wood against her back an instant before he tucked her in his arms. But mostly she could feel him. Surrounding her. Loving her. And it felt so right to be loved by him.

Rhys, she thought, unaware as she fell into an exhausted sleep that she'd spoken the name out loud.

5

Dalton's Magic Rule #6:
Seize Every Opportunity To Perform.

"You are so hot. I want to do you over and over again."

Melina smiled at Rhys's raspy voice, but didn't bother to respond since her mouth was busy doing other things and didn't appear interested in giving up the warm flesh it was sucking on. Instead, she hummed her appreciation for the remark, smiling even more when he groaned.

"I can never get enough of you, Melina. Never, do you understand?" His fingers tangled in her hair and pulled. "Look at me."

Just for kicks, she resisted and sucked him harder. She swirled her tongue around his broad, mushroom tip, then flattened it against the sensitive spot just below his slit. He hissed in a breath. Rhys fisted her hair more tightly and tugged, forcing her to release him even as she moaned in protest.

"You hog the covers, Ladybug."

Melina's eyes snapped open and, for a moment, her dream and reality vied for supremacy.

Reality: Her vision was just as it should be without her glasses and first thing in the morning, a little fuzzy but not enough to prevent her from seeing that there was a man lying next to her. A big, naked man.

Dream: The man was Rhys, his head propped on his bent arm.   A joy she'd never experienced slammed into her, but then disappeared almost immediately when reality took the lead.

She hadn't been going down on Rhys. He hadn't wrapped her hair around his fists. And, thankfully, he certainly hadn't called her a hog.

Little comfort there.

This was Max, she remembered. And as much as she loved and adored Max, he wasn't Rhys and he never would be. She could never feel the same way about—

Her eyes widened in horror just as he reached out and ran a finger down the slope of her bare shoulder. The events of the night before rushed her like a linebacker in the final inning of a playoff game. Or was that hockey? Baseball? She didn't know any more about sports than she did about magic. Still, she knew that last night hadn't gone exactly as she'd planned.

Not her plan, anyway.

She sucked in a breath as Max's hand slipped under the sheet to cover one of her bare breasts. Just as they had last night, her nipples came to immediate attention, tightening as if to reach out for his fingers. Teasingly, he grazed one, then the other, before he lightly began rubbing one in tiny, firm circles. When she gasped, he smiled. "You're sensitive there. I noticed that last night."

Dumbstruck, she just stared at him. She never would have thought it was true, but he apparently brought something out in her. Maybe one too many solo test runs had triggered some kind of latent chemical reaction in her? Why else would she have been so heated in her response last night? With Max, she reminded herself.

But present circumstances didn't prove her theory. She'd slept through the night—after three screaming orgasms—and she was still raring to go. Apparently, so was he.

Her eyes widened as another thought struck her. He was raring to go because he hadn't come. She hadn't gotten him off. She jerked to a sitting position, barely clutching the sheet before it exposed her bare chest to the world. "Oh, God. I knew it. Brian was right. I do suck in bed. And not," she held up a hand to forestall his anticipated attempt at humor, "in a good way."

Drawing up her knees, she buried her face in them and covered her head with her arms. She struggled to block out all stimuli and simply think. Even so, she felt him stiffen next to her. His words, when they came, didn't sound humorous in the least. "The bastard told you that and you believed him? You still do? After last night?"

She jerked her face up to look at him. "Of course after last night," she hissed, poking him in the chest with her finger. "You proved it."

"Excuse me?" Grabbing hold of her finger, he leaned in toward her, nose to nose, until she could clearly see his fierce frown. Anger emanated from him in waves. "All we proved last night was you are capable of far more passion than you thought. I've got the claw marks and the ringing ears to prove it."

Flushing, she jerked her finger away and buried her face in her knees again. Her next words came out muffled and garbled. "Also proofs incisor golden bat."

"What?"

She lifted her head again and spoke past the hair that had tangled in her mouth. "All that proved is that you're good in bed," she clarified. "We already knew that. I, on the other hand, am a flop. I just didn't accept it before."

He shook his head and spat out, "Bullshit." Despite the fury in his voice, his hand was gentle as he smoothed back the hair from her face. "Melina, what are you talking about? Last night was the best—"

"You didn't get off," she yelled. "We agreed that you were going to teach me about pleasing a man, and instead you drove me so wild that I...that I—" She shook her head.

"Finish." His voice had turned quiet, almost icy. He also moved away from her, just a foot or two, but it was enough to make her feel the rejection. Great, now he was angry. But why shouldn't he be? She'd barely touched him last night. Sure, he'd ordered her not to, but maybe that had been some kind of challenge. Some test to see if she was aggressive enough to give him what he really wanted?

"I-I was selfish. I completely forgot about what I should be doing for you, Max. But it was only because you were so...you were so much more—" So much more than she'd expected. Based on that kiss so long ago, she'd thought she'd be safe with Max. It had been nice, but it hadn't overwhelmed her. It hadn't affected her the way just thinking of Rhys did. It hadn't made her tremble, but she was trembling now. When her face was buried in her knees and she consciously remembered who he was, she could control the ripples of desire that were swirling inside her. But as soon as she lifted her head and saw him—as soon as she breathed him in—the drumbeats of a passion so momentous began to clamor in her ears, urging her to reach out to him.

"What was I, Melina?"

Pressing her lips together, she plucked at the bedspread, refusing to look at him.

"You came into my bed," Rhys said. "Apparently, you arranged all this for one of your idiotic experiments. So you will look at me, damn you." Gripping her chin, he turned her face toward him, not unkindly, but not gently either. "What was I? Who am I?"

She frowned. "What?"

"Who. Am. I?"

"You—" She squinted, but the picture didn't change. He was Max. Honey-colored hair, slightly shorter than she remembered from two days before, but he could have gotten a haircut. Strong nose and jaw. Broad shoulders and chest, enticingly bare. Automatically, her gaze dropped lower and she saw his bare limbs splayed out from underneath the stark white sheet. She couldn't see the light dusting of hair on them, but she'd felt it last night. When he'd lain on top of her, with her wrists manacled by his hands—

She sucked in a breath and held it. Along with a flash of her favorite fantasy, two memories from last night formed. The first, his seeming surprise when he'd come into the room and found her in his bed. She'd chalked it up to nerves, but had it been more? The second, he'd called her Ladybug. Only Rhys called her Ladybug. But Rhys wasn't here. He didn't even like her anymore. Plus, he wouldn't have known to come to her. Unless…

"Rhys?" she whispered. Already half-expecting his answer, she rose and pulled the sheet up with her. His expression flashed with confirmation.

"Melina," he said warningly, grabbing for the sheet, but she moved quick and with desperation, winning the tug of war so she could back up toward the door. And do what? Run out naked into the hallway? Prove herself to be an even bigger idiot? She compensated by taking a side-step toward the open bathroom doorway.

He stood, unconcerned with his nudity. "Come here, Ladybug," he said quietly.

She shook her head. "You're Max. Tell me you're Max."

He crossed his arms over his chest, standing proud

and tall. "I'm sorry. I can't do that."

With her one free hand, she covered her mouth to stifle her moan of horror. She felt her knees about to buckle and put a steadying hand on the wall. She'd needed to steady herself on the bed last night, she remembered. She'd thought it was because she wasn't wearing her glasses, but it had more likely been because of the alcohol. The alcohol that had emboldened her to climb into the bed and masturbate while she fantasized about Rhys while actually thinking that she could go to bed with his brother. All in the interest of science, of course.

And what she'd done instead was throw herself at Rhys. Begged him to please her, she remembered with mortification. What had she said? *Please me. Suck me.*

"Melina," he began again.

She shook her head. Now that she knew, it seemed so obvious. His hair was shorter. He spoke more slowly. He touched her differently. More hesitantly.

More and more hesitantly as time went on.

Except for last night.

A slicing pain tugged at her stomach, and she automatically clutched at it. His surprise last night had been just that. He hadn't been expecting her to throw herself at him. He'd gone along, probably to spare her feelings. It certainly wasn't because he'd been overcome by desire. He hadn't even tried to seek his own release. Maybe he'd already known he couldn't achieve that kind of satisfaction with her. Maybe Max had warned him.

Now a hollow feeling of betrayal burned along with

her embarrassment and heartache. "Whose room is this?"

"Mine."

"Not Max's?"

"Max is on a different floor."

A different floor. So had the front desk made a mistake? Or had Max chickened out at the last minute and tricked Rhys into filling in for him?

That made the most sense.

Despite her brief suspicion that Max had told Rhys she was waiting for him, the evidence didn't point to him purposefully deceiving her. When she'd said his brother's name, he'd sounded displeased—with her, with his brother, with the entire situation.

"Why…what…what are you doing here?"

"I flew in to give you your birthday present. It's right on the dresser. Didn't you see it?" Holding out his hands as if she was a rabid dog about to bite him, he nevertheless took two steps toward her, skirting the bed much like she had the night before. She moved backward, matching him step for step, suddenly feeling like a tiny rabbit being stalked by a very hungry wolf. "You gave me a present instead. Too bad it wasn't meant for me, but—"

"But nothing," she said. "You need to leave."

He swept his hands down his tall, muscular form. "You're going to make me walk out of here naked?"

"You can-you can dress first. While I shower."

Another step forward by him. Another step back for her. "Let's talk."

Talk. What was there to talk about other than her

wanting to die from humiliation? "You weren't expecting me."

He froze and seemed to weigh his words carefully before answering. "No, but—"

"You didn't want this."

"Now, that's not true."

She laughed even as she swiped at the tears gathered in her eyes. "Oh, is that why you've been hounding me with so much attention? Who are you dating now, Rhys? I bet she looks just like me, doesn't she?"

The look that flashed across his face was subtle, but she caught it. She remembered the picture on her bookcase. The one where he posed with a woman Hugh Hefner would've been proud of. She'd had Barbie-like dimensions. Thirty-eight double D's if she wasn't mistaken. Melina was barely a B-cup, and her hourglass shape was bottom heavy. She probably wouldn't have been allowed to clean the Playboy mansion, let alone live there.

As she came even with the open bathroom doorway, he shook his head. "Melina, please, don't—"

"Just go," she whispered.

She saw him tense, saw him shift on the balls of his feet and knew he was going to lunge for her. But he was too far away. He'd never make it in time. Which is why he cursed when she propelled herself into the bathroom, shut the door and locked it.

The heavy thump of a fist against the door made her flinch, but he didn't call out to her. He did mutter a slow, steady stream of cuss words that would have amused her if she hadn't been so devastated. Rhys had plenty of surprises up his sleeves, including a kinky side and hot temper. Slowly, she sank to the floor, crawled under the open space of the double sink, and curled into a corner.

No matter what he said, he hadn't wanted her. That open box of condoms hadn't been for her.

And now she was stuck in this bathroom, with her overnight bag still on the floor outside, with no clothes. No pride. And no hope. She wasn't strong enough to risk this kind of hurt again. She wasn't ever going to be able to please a man, and that included Jamie. When Rhys left, she would get dressed and drive home. Then she'd throw herself into her work instead of silly dreams of a family and children.

Right after she killed Max.

* * *

His gaze never leaving the closed bathroom door, Rhys tugged on fresh clothes, cursing the whole time. She'd thought he was Max. When she'd offered to please him. When he'd kissed her. When he'd lain on top of her, played with her nipples, had his fingers and tongue inside her. She'd thought he was his brother.

Hurt and anger fought for supremacy. He wanted to rip his brother apart. Wanted to yell at her for daring to ask his brother for such a stupid, idiotic, lame-brained, ridiculous, personal, intimate favor.

She sucked in bed? She'd believed her asshole of an ex-boyfriend so much that she'd sought out tutoring lessons on how to pleasure a man? From Max?

Raking his hands through his hair, he stopped staring at the door long enough to pace. And his brother had agreed, only to back out in the end. It didn't take a rocket scientist to figure out that, given their conversation at the theater and in the bar last night, he'd thought to pave the way for Rhys. He couldn't decide whether to beat the shit out of Max or kiss his feet in gratitude.

Pausing, he took a deep breath and sat on the bed. He eyed Melina's overnight case and knew she wouldn't come out of the bathroom until she thought he was gone. Grabbing the overnight case, he thought about throwing it down the hallway. Instead, he shoved it under the desk, out of view. He wasn't going to make leaving him easy for her.

Falling back on the bed, he stared at the ceiling and allowed himself to process things. He was upset, yes, but he was also thinking clearheadedly now, something he obviously hadn't been doing when Melina had been standing in her underwear in front of him last night.

His clearheaded thinking was one of the things that made the act with his brother work. Off stage, Max was clearly the more extroverted. His passion and enthusiasm for performing were what pumped up Rhys's genuine but more quiet interest in magic. Unlike his brother, Rhys wasn't impulsive. Ever. He thought things through, whether it was the believability of a magic trick, what position in the room gave him the best advantage when it came to illusion, or whether a woman was hitting on him for his fame rather than a true interest in the man he was.

While there were more of the former than the latter, that didn't necessarily mean he'd turn a woman down just because she liked the limelight. He just liked to know what he was getting into from the beginning. That way, he maintained control from beginning to end, just like with his magic.

He decided what people saw and didn't see.

He made things happen.

But not with Melina. He'd never had that kind of control with her, and that more than anything else was probably what had kept him away from her. If he couldn't even control his feelings for her, what made him think that if he ever had her, he'd be able to leave? And leaving was always what he and his brother did. It was in their blood. He couldn't imagine staying in one place, day after day, month after month, working the same job. Even for Melina.

Or, more precisely, he could imagine it, but he couldn't accept such bliss was actually possible. Not on his part. And not on hers.

The first thing he'd thought when she'd called him Max was, "Not again." He loved his brother, but sometimes he felt like he lived in his shadow. That no one truly saw him for who he was because they were always a pair.

The only thing that stopped him from freaking out

completely was the fact she'd said his name last night, right after he'd undeniably given her the best orgasms of her life. Her defenses had been down, and she clearly hadn't realized Max hadn't shown up.

But she'd still said his name.

That meant a lot. Right now, that meant everything.

His right shoulder itched with intuition just before the phone rang. Rolling over, he reached for the phone and picked it up, knowing immediately who it was. "You are so dead."

Silence. Then a hesitant, "Where's Melina?"

"Listen, you little—"

"If that's your brother," Melina yelled from the bathroom, "you can tell him he's a dead man when I see him."

"Already done, Ladybug," he called through clenched teeth.

"She's still there?" Max sounded so proud of himself that Rhys tightened his hand on the receiver, wishing it was his brother's neck. "So what's the problem, man? I'm assuming you took advantage of the situation?"

"That's the problem, Max. I don't take advantage of women, especially not Melina."

"So you didn't—" His brother cleared his throat. "You know?"

"No. Why don't you enlighten me? Exactly what did you think was going to happen, Max?"

"Was she wearing something sexy?"

Rhys remembered the little shorts and top she had

been wearing, modest and simple by most standards, and currently lying on the floor. "Flannel pajamas."

"Damn. And her hair?"

Loose and gorgeous. Feeling more relaxed, Rhys stretched out on the bed only to tense when he heard the bathroom door unclick. Feigning disinterest, he stayed on the bed as Melina peeked out from around the corner, her hands clutching her sheet while she searched for the bag he'd moved underneath the desk. "Pinned back in that bun of hers."

"And the glasses?" Max groaned.

"The glasses? As butt-ugly as ever." He looked straight at her when he said it, and she wrinkled her nose and stuck out her tongue at him. He sat up, and her eyes widened, which, bastard that he was, immediately made him hard. Despite the fact he was fully clothed, he didn't miss the way her gaze moved down then up his body. Unlike similar glances other women gave him, her hesitant assessment made his chest puff out and his heart pound out of control.

"So what the hell did you guys do all night?"

"What do you think we did? We played rummy, watched a girly movie, and I ended up sleeping on the floor."

Melina covered her mouth to hide her smile of relief, but he saw it anyway. He cocked an eyebrow at her.

"No sparks?"

More like Mount St. Helens. "Not a one."

Max sighed. "Well, hey, I'm sorry, man. I really

87

thought...I don't know. I just thought if I finally pushed the two of you into taking a chance—"

Almost feeling sorry for his brother now, Rhys smiled and rose. "You're still dead when I see you."

"So Melina's okay?"

His smile widened until a grin split his face. While she remained frozen where she stood, wrapped in the sheet like a Grecian goddess, both determination and anticipation rolled through him. He stared at her. What he might have done or should have done before no longer mattered. She'd offered herself to him. She wanted sexual tutoring? Fine. Mistake or not, he was definitely the best man for the job. He was going to prove both her and that little twerp she'd dated wrong. By the time he was through with her, she'd know exactly the kind of power she held over a man. Over him.

"She's going to be fine." Dropping his gaze, he allowed himself to take in the curves he'd felt and tasted last night. He wanted that sheet gone. Now. And by the way she was looking at him, she was starting to realize it. "In fact, she's going to be fucking fabulous."

While his brother squawked and started asking questions, Rhys hung up on him. He planted his hands on his hips and thrust his jaw out aggressively. "You ready for your next lesson, Ladybug?"

Game on.

* * *

Melina stared at Rhys and shifted uneasily from one foot to the other.

Next lesson? Was he crazy or was she? Because suddenly she wanted to drop her sheet, wrap herself around him, and never let go.

Fortunately for her, her saner side prevailed. After three failed relationships, she didn't believe it was better to love and lose, rather than never to have loved before. Especially not with Rhys. She loved him. She'd always loved him. But that love, combined with his pulling away from her, had caused her far too much pain of late.

If she was honest with herself, Rhys had hurt her far worse than Brian ever could, and that was not something she was going to ignore. If she held any place in his heart still, she'd have to content herself with that; she wasn't going to voluntarily seek out more only to have him walk away from her again. She turned toward the bathroom. "Um, I think I'll—"

"I feel it only fair to warn you that if you try to hide in the bathroom again, I'll just have to break the door down."

Surprise came first, then she couldn't help it. She laughed. She laughed long and hard. When she finally managed to control herself and look at him, he was frowning fiercely.

"Glad to know the idea of me exerting enough strength to break down a door amuses you."

It was the idea of him exerting such effort for her that had made her laugh, but she didn't tell him that. Shaking her head, she bit her lip. "I'm sorry. It's not that. I just...I just laugh when I'm nervous." Plus, Rhys had just told Max what he normally thought of her. With her, men expected flannel pajamas, pinned-back hair, butt-ugly glasses.

Weren't those the same words Max had used to describe her choice in eye decor?

Even as she appreciated his discretion, she wondered if it was because he was too embarrassed to admit that he'd actually done anything with her. The thought pierced a tender spot inside her, when she'd thought she'd guarded those softer places long ago.

"So I make you nervous? Why is that, do you think?"

Any trace of humor slipped, and she averted her gaze. So he knew he made her nervous. Big deal. Like he hadn't already figured that out a long time ago with the way she always flushed and stuttered around him. "Can you give me my overnight bag? I thought I left it—"

"I gave it to a passing bellboy while you were in the bathroom."

She narrowed her eyes at him. "You did not."

He shrugged. "No, I didn't. But I did hide it. I don't want you getting dressed and rushing out of here before we talk."

"But that's...that's—" she sputtered.

"Childish? Hey, desperate times and all that. But if you want to look around, then by all means..." He waved his hand in invitation.

For a moment, she just stared at him. What was motivating him to be so difficult about this? He had to know she was embarrassed about the mix-up, yet he was forcing her to confront him. Why wouldn't he just let it go? Why was he getting so much pleasure from her humiliation?

The answer came to her so suddenly that she felt foolish for not thinking of it sooner. This was obviously about the competitive male ego. He was probably offended that she'd asked Max for the favor and not him. Well, he didn't need any more ego stroking from her. Her performance last night should have already told him that she was putty in his hands.

She glanced around but didn't see her bag anywhere. Her purse, however, was by the television. Next to his cologne and that box of condoms. She snatched her purse, rifled through it, and found her spare glasses. With a mutinous thrust of her chin, she put them on. Her vision immediately focused, making her feel slightly calmer. "Honestly, Rhys," she said, trying to sound bemused. "I don't know why you won't just give me my bag. All I want is my clothes."

"Because seeing you all naked and pink and wearing nothing but those glasses would give me enormous pleasure." He stepped closer to her and tugged playfully at the sheet that she clutched with whitened knuckles. "Lots of men dream of being taken by the prim librarian who's really a wildcat in bed. That's what this is all about, right? Learning how to please a man? I think we established last night that I qualify as a member of the male species. At least by touch. Would you like to see the proof itself?"

His hands hovered over the button fly of his jeans.

"You're not funny."

He smiled and shrugged. "Funny is the last thing I'm trying to be."

She pondered what he'd said. "Do men really fantasize about librarians? I would have thought the average male liked something more overt. That's why porn flicks and skin magazines are so popular, isn't it?"

Now it was his turn to erupt in laughter. "Skin magazines?"

"What? That's what they're called, aren't they?"

"Sure, by some people. I just never thought to hear that term coming from your pretty lips."

The casual compliment made her blush, but she immediately batted the pleasure it caused away. "Oh, you view me as asexual?"

In an instant, his expression grew serious. Heated. "I've never thought of you as asexual. Not by a long shot and certainly not after last night. Honey, you've got more passion in you than most men could handle."

"Most, but not you, right?"

"I think I 'handled' you pretty well last night." Reaching out, he gripped her chin between his thumb and forefinger, refusing to let her turn away. "Now, why don't you tell me what possessed you to go to Max in the first place? Your ex sold you a bill of goods, Melina, and I would think you're way too smart to fall for it."

Too smart? Yes, that was her. Her brain told her that Brian was just an insecure man with an average-size penis that needed to "diss" her in order to feel more manly. But her bruised heart—the heart that longed to find love and companionship and family—told her that it was her own fault she was alone. Which meant admitting to herself that Brian was actually right. She *had* lain there like a board half the time. Because she'd never felt inspired to do otherwise. Until last night. "Why didn't you tell Max what happened when he called?"

"Because what happens between you and me has nothing to do with him."

He looked so fierce, so possessive, that she shivered. "In this case, it did. He tricked you, didn't he?"

"He didn't trick me. He just didn't tell me what was waiting for me."

"And if he had?"

"If he had, I wouldn't have waited for you to do your little fashion spin. I would have been on top of you before the door shut."

Her entire body responded to his quiet statement. Her skin prickled, her nipples peaked, and her pussy wept. She would've sworn that if he were to touch her hair at that moment, she would come so hard she'd probably black out. She urged her mind to quiet the urges of her body and be logical. "Liar," she whispered. "You haven't called. You haven't visited. You haven't wanted anything to do with me."

"Not because I didn't want you." He hesitated. "You didn't exactly advertise that you wanted me."

"I-I didn't—"

"Don't lie," he commanded, cupping the back of her head and pulling her in to his chest. Stunned, she closed her eyes and soaked him in. With a slow, firm hand, he rubbed her lower back. "We've lied to each other enough, don't you think? You might have picked Max to be your tutor, but it was my name you said before you fell asleep last night. And I want you, Melina. I'm willing to say it. I'm willing to act on it."

She leaned back to meet his gaze, doubt and suspicion boiling inside her. "Why now? After all this time?"

"Because you offered it to me."

"I pushed it on you."

"That's a stupid thing to say, and you're not stupid."

"Yes, well, here's where my stupidity ends." Pulling away, she urged, "If you'll just get me my clothes, I'll get out of here."

"Why? You were willing to sleep with Max. Was it because you love him?"

"No! I mean, of course, I love him, the same way I love you. We're family. I don't want to ruin that, Rhys, and what you're talking about will. Admit it. We want different things in our lives and trying to pretend otherwise would be foolish."

He didn't contradict her. How could he? "You and Max want different things, too. Why were you willing to let him teach you but not me?"

Ah, so she'd been right. This was about his male ego. "Because he was around, for one."

"I'm here now. And I've got the weekend, just like

you and Max agreed, right?"

Alarm bells blared in her head. "Yes, but—"

"And I think we established last night that we have chemistry. That I have the skill to make you come." He said it quietly, with none of the cockiness that would have made her question her attraction to him.

Instead, Melina struggled to breathe in the rapidly thinning air. "Your skill has never been in question. And my ability to…to—" She felt herself turning beet red. "—climax isn't in issue. It's my ability to pleasure a man that is."

"Says you."

"Says Brian Montgomery. Lars Jensen. Gary Somada."

"Idiots. If they wanted something from you, they didn't work hard enough for it. Besides, I can show you how to please a man."

"You seemed more concerned with pleasing me last night."

"The two things aren't independent. I showed you one thing that gives a man pleasure. Submission. Total trust by his partner. But there are other things you can do, and I'll show them to you if you'll let me."

The alarm in her head was still sounding, but somehow it had quieted a bit. Curiosity, she told herself. That's all. She wasn't actually going to consider his proposition. Was she?

At her continued silence, he pressed on. "Don't get me wrong. I'm not immune to some satisfaction, as well.

I put in some work last night. I think I'm entitled to a little return on my investment, don't you?"

Her alarm kicked up a notch. "So this is about paying a debt owed? Compensating you for services rendered?"

"This is about you and me and giving each other the best sex we've ever had."

"See? That's exactly it. If you're expecting great sex from me, it'll never work. I'll be anxious. Feel pressured. You're deluding yourself if you think I can compete with the women you've been with, Rhys."

He raised a brow. "And you're underestimating my ability to inspire you."

Okay. Her curiosity was definitely getting the better of her now. Melina forced herself not to think of Rhys's special brand of inspiration. "We barely know each other anymore—"

"You know that's not true. Like you said, Melina, we're almost family. What we're doing this weekend might not fit within the boundaries of our previous relationship, but once it's over, I want to know you're going to be okay. I can help you. Why won't you let me?"

Once it's over, he'd said. Once he was gone, he meant. A wave of sadness washed over her. If she understood him correctly, this was to be their swan song to whatever relationship they'd been clinging to. Sort of like his parting gift to her. Since it had been coming for a while, she tried not to show how much the thought devastated her. Or swayed her.

As soon as the weekend was over, he'd be leaving

again. Who knew when she'd see him next? She'd be a fool not to take what he was offering.

"And then what?" she forced herself to ask, even though she already knew the answer.

"What were you going to do after you and Max were done with each other?"

It seemed obscene somehow, the way he kept bringing Max into this. Which was silly, of course. "We were going to part friends. Go back to the way things always were. No expectations. No embarrassment."

He seemed to hesitate for a moment, then said, "I can do that. Can you?"

Given his cavalier attitude, what else could she say? Slowly, she nodded.

Satisfaction gleamed in his eyes. "Good."

He moved forward and she tensed, expecting him to reach out and kiss her. Anticipation streaked through her, but all he did was turn, bend his knees slightly, and retrieve a familiar-looking bag from under the desk. He tossed it onto the bed next to her. "Now get dressed."

She stared at the bag blankly. "Now you want me to get dressed?"

He smiled slightly. "Yep."

"Why?"

He cocked an eyebrow at her. "Because, my dear Melina, the next lesson involves something the best magicians and lovers know how to work with a very subtle yet sure hand."

"What's that?" she whispered.

"Unpredictability."

6

Dalton's Magic Rule #7:
Don't forget your magic wand.

As he turned Melina's car onto the freeway that would lead them north of Sacramento, Rhys had to struggle not to show his amusement. Although she was valiantly trying to act nonchalant, he'd definitely thrown her off balance. And if he was reading her correctly, and Rhys had a definite talent when it came to reading people, she was a bit disgruntled that she was fully clothed going who knows where instead of enjoying more time in his arms and in his bed.

Which was exactly the response he'd been hoping for.

He hadn't been lying when he'd told her that unpredictability was key to good magic and good sex. It was also the key to getting Melina to lower her guard and stop those gigantic wheels in her mind from trying to analyze everything to death. God knew, if he was going to participate in her ridiculous sex experiment, he was going to enjoy every second of their time together.

He wanted the same for her. He wanted her relaxed and with her guard down, enjoying their time together instead of focusing on things like technique and statistics—each orgasm used as a marker of sexual prowess.

He almost snorted.

She actually thought she sucked in bed because he hadn't allowed himself release when the truth was he'd found more sexual pleasure giving her orgasms and having her sleep in his arms than he had in a long time. He hadn't been willing to go for the fast finish or self-induced hand job, because he'd wanted more with her. More kissing. More touching. More.

And now he'd have the opportunity, but only because she'd gotten it into her head that she needed tutoring. Ridiculous, but he wasn't going to look a gift horse in the mouth. Not this time.

She cleared her throat. "So, where are we going?" she asked, as if he hadn't already refused to answer her the four other times she'd asked.

He turned to look at her with a carefree grin. "That wouldn't exactly keep the mystery going now, would it?"

She pouted so adorably that he barely stopped himself from grabbing her chin and pulling her over for a kiss. It didn't take a genius to figure out that his Ladybug instinctively resisted anything that she couldn't control. He obviously needed to steer her mind to safer ground.

"How're your parents, by the way?"

The question wiped the pout off her mouth, and she sat back. "They're good. They're in China now, checking out the Great Wall."

"We were there a couple of years ago. It was an amazing trip. They've been traveling for the last couple of years, right? And things are still good between them?"

"Sure, why wouldn't they be?"

He thought of all the fights his parents had gotten into while on the road, just another thing he'd had to learn to adjust to. "It's a miracle that my parents' marriage survived their touring. Sometimes I think they brought us along with them as a buffer just to keep their marriage intact."

She shifted slightly in her seat, turning closer toward him instead of continuing to hug the door. "But your parents seem so compatible. I don't think I've ever seen them fight."

He couldn't help his smirk. "Yes, but you only saw them at home. They're completely different on the road. You ever see that show *The Amazing Race*?"

"Sure. I love it actually. You're not saying…"

"All those pairs trying to navigate around foreign countries under intense pressure—that doesn't exactly bring out the best in them, right? Well, let's just say my mom shows a whole different side of herself when she's tired or hungry. And my dad seems to lose his ability to read her when he's distracted and on the road."

"Was that hard for you? That they fought a lot?"

It had been, at one time. Until he'd realized it was just

part of his parents' process. They fought on the road, and probably made up just as fiercely. Once he'd realized their love was solid enough to withstand the fighting, he'd stopped stressing about it. He, on the other hand, wasn't willing to put up with that kind of strife in his personal relationships.

"Rhys?"

Melina reached out and took his hand, giving it a gentle squeeze. Affection washed over him. Melina was such a doll, with a generous heart and fierce loyalty. She would make some lucky guy a wonderful wife, some child a wonderful mother. For a moment, disappointment that he wouldn't be that husband, and that it wouldn't be their child, spiked through him. He squeezed her hand back and shot her a quick smile. "Sorry. I spaced there for a second. What did you ask?"

"How are they doing now?"

"They're learning to enjoy one another again, but they're still on the road with us about half the time. Dad's our manager, you know, and Mom's mentored each of our female stage assistants. They'll always be part of the act in that way."

"Is that a drag for you and Max, when they're with you?"

He frowned when she pulled her hand away. When he glanced at her, she was looking out the window and blushing. His eyebrows shot up. Just what was his little Ladybug referring to? "Not at all. Why?"

"I can't imagine it's conducive to—" She waved her

hand in a yada-yada circle. "You have a lot of women interested in you on the road. I'm not naïve enough to think that you don't take advantage of it."

Internally, he winced. The last thing he wanted to discuss with Melina was his sex life, but because she was brave enough to ask, he forced himself to be honest. "It's hard not to. There are a lot of willing women. But it got old for me pretty quickly. Believe it or not, I'm often relieved when my parents are on tour with us. Gives me a great excuse to bow out of the nightlife and just hang with them."

"It's nice," she said wistfully, turning to face him again. "The relationship that you have with them."

"What about your parents?" He hesitated, then asked the question he never thought he would. "Would you ever want to join them on the road?"

"They wouldn't want me to."

He jerked in surprise. "You can't be serious. Your parents have always adored you. How can you say that?"

"Oh, I didn't mean that the way it sounded. Outwardly, they'd welcome me. But, really, I'd be a third wheel. I know they love me, but there's a bond between them. They wouldn't want me around."

"Seriously?"

"It was only after I was grown and out of the house that my parents started traveling. Maybe that's when they truly felt they could be a couple. So I try not to intrude. Plus, I don't enjoy traveling all that much. It takes me away from work, and I like having a home base."

More proof that he wasn't the right man for Melina. He didn't have a home base. Didn't even know what having one would feel like anymore.

He was tempted to ask her how much traveling she'd done. As far as he knew, she hadn't done much, and he'd always assumed that had been her choice. Now he wasn't so sure. Now he wondered if it was just that she hadn't wanted to travel alone. But it seemed to be a topic she didn't want to continue. And he wasn't sure he wanted to continue it either, given the melancholy look that had come across her face. "Once you were on your own, I thought your mom might start acting again."

Melina's mother had been an up-and-coming actress right around the time she'd met Melina's father. Years ago, he'd rented one of her movies, amazed at how animated she'd been. Whenever he'd seen her as a kid, she'd been friendly but quiet. Serious. Far from the chirpy, flirty girl on the screen. Although she hadn't been as quiet or serious as a child, Melina had slowly adopted those traits as she'd grown up, and he'd felt more and more separated from her. He now wondered which of her mother's personas had been real versus an act. He already knew that Melina's quiet exterior hid something amazingly passionate, but that was a new discovery made only last night.

"No. She gave that world up a long time ago. She loved my father that much."

Rhys wasn't sure why giving up her acting dreams was part and parcel of being with Melina's father, but he had to admit they were a good pairing. It was, in fact, hard to believe that Susan, Melina's mother, had ever been in show business. She'd adapted to academic life as if she'd been born to it. Their relationship had been completely different than Rhys's parents' because there didn't seem to be a lot of volatility to it. Melina's parents always worked together in sync, similar personalities that managed to converge into one unit. For the first time, he wondered exactly how it would feel to be the outsider in that relationship, when a daughter shouldn't ever be made to feel like an outsider. But that was clearly how Melina felt.

"So these willing women. How do they let their willingness be known?"

Something close to panic shot through him. "Um...I don't think we should really talk about that."

"Why not? You now know intimate details about my sex life while I know nothing about yours."

"All I know is that, up until last night, your choice in lovers was lousy."

"Are you referring to your brother? Because I didn't exactly choose you, did I?"

He didn't miss the way she kept bringing up Max. She was using him as a shield, just as she had many times in the past. "You're here now, aren't you? And considering what we're going to be doing for the next two days, I'd say that you've definitely made a choice. Or have you changed your mind?"

She hesitated long enough for him to begin to sweat. Don't change your mind, he urged silently. *Not when I've only had a taste of what I've dreamed about for so long.*

"No," she whispered. "I haven't changed my mind. Not if you haven't. But I am here for a reason. So that means you have to answer my questions."

Frustration made him clench his teeth, but he slowly relaxed his jaw. "It's usually a note passed to us by an usher. Sometimes they'll wait around until we're leaving the theater. One time—" He cleared his throat, then forced himself to be honest. "One woman actually found out where we were staying and walked up while I was having dinner. She, uh, made it pretty clear she wasn't wearing anything under her trench coat. Then she said she had a message for me. Drawn on her body with lipstick."

Silence filled the car for several minutes, and he struggled for something to say. Screw honesty. He should have kept that last one to himself. "So, why don't we—"

"Well, the lipstick was certainly...overt. But that's what guys like, right? Did it work? Did you end up having sex with her?"

He tightened his fingers on the steering wheel. Without taking his eyes off the road, he answered quietly. "Yes. But that was a long time ago. When I was still reeling from the attention and thinking with my dick more than my brain."

"Did she really have something written on her body with lipstick?"

He glanced over at her. "Yes."

Her eyes widened and she blushed. "Was it something...explicit?"

Sighing, he shrugged. "Let's just say it involved an

arrow and two short words."

"Did you do what it said?" she whispered.

"No."

"Why not?"

How could he explain that he simply he hadn't wanted to? That he never did unless he knew the woman well. Cared about her. Yet he'd had sex with her. It sounded so distasteful now. Made him cringe to imagine what Melina must think of him.

Before he could reply, she said, "I bet she went down on you, though, right?"

He gritted his teeth, then willed his muscles to relax. As much as he wanted to be for Melina, he'd never claimed to be perfect. If she was going to be with him, it would be all of him, flaws and all. Still, he didn't want to spend any more of their precious time together talking about something he barely even remembered now. So in his own way, that's what he set out to tell her. "Honestly, that entire night's pretty much a big blur now. One big red blur of Shanghai Crimson. Revlon, I believe."

Holding his breath, he kept his gaze on the road. She was silent for so long, he finally turned and looked at her. Her face was blank of emotion, and he expected her to launch into a lecture about safe sex or women's rights. Instead, she burst out laughing.

Relieved, he reached out to caress her leg. She stiffened, and her gaze immediately locked onto his hand. He stroked her in a soft, soothing motion. "Like I said, that was a long time ago, Melina. I'm much more discerning about who I'm with now."

Her expression grew serious. "Unless it's an old friend who's sneaked into your hotel room."

"*Especially* when it's an old friend who's sneaked into my hotel room. Believe me, seeing you lying in my bed turned me on more than that woman ever did."

"You don't have to—"

He squeezed her knee warningly. "I'm serious."

She shrugged. "Sure. Whatever."

Turning back to the window, she clearly communicated that their conversation was over. He let her shut him out for a bit, but he kept his hand on her leg, reminding her with his touch that he wasn't going anywhere.

About thirty minutes later, he caught the yawn she tried to stifle. "We're going on a bit of a drive. Why don't you go ahead and go to sleep?"

She shook her head. "I can keep you company."

"You will be keeping me company. Besides, you're going to need your rest."

Her eyes rounded. "What are we going to do?"

He shot her a wicked grin. "Patience, baby. I'll reveal the class outline when we get to where we're going."

She narrowed her eyes at him. "Are you trying to be funny?"

He slid his hand just a fraction higher on her leg, and she gasped. Just as he'd hoped, she reached out and grabbed his hand with her own. Satisfied, he tightened his hold on hers, resting their linked hands on her knee. "Just rest. I promise, you'll know everything in just a couple of hours."

For a moment, their gazes held, and he brought her hand up to his mouth to kiss it. "Now close those beautiful eyes and sleep, Ladybug."

He almost chuckled out loud at the way her eyes widened again. Leaning her head back, she stared at him while he focused on the road. He felt her gaze on him and rubbed his thumb in slow, circular movements against the back of her hand. Within minutes, he felt her begin to relax. Within ten, she'd closed her eyes. And within twenty, her soft, steady breathing told him she'd gone to sleep.

Gently, he brought their raised hands back to his lips for another soft kiss.

* * *

When Melina awoke, she was in the passenger seat of her car, and she was alone. Jolting up, she frantically searched for Rhys and immediately saw him standing near the front of the car, talking to a bearded man in a baseball cap. Pulling down the visor, she checked herself in the mirror, wincing at the sight that looked back at her.

Her glasses were askew, her hair limp, no makeup on her face. But the men had turned toward her, and Rhys was motioning her outside and she'd feel like an absolute fool if she didn't go out and greet them. So she straightened her glasses, took a deep breath, and opened the car.

"Melina, this is my friend, Rod. He owns the Holiday Harbor store." Rhys gestured to the weathered, two-story building behind them. Beyond it, a long dock floated over a peaceful lake surrounded by tall redwood trees. "Rod, this is Melina."

She held out her hand. "A pleasure to meet you."

"The pleasure's all mine." Ignoring her proffered hand, Rod pulled her in for a deep bear hug. "It's great to finally meet you. I've heard a lot about you from the Dalton family over the years."

Flushed with pleasure, Melina smoothed back her hair. "Th-that's nice." She peeked up at Rhys, and he tucked his hand around her waist and pulled her closer. At first, she held herself slightly apart from him as he continued to talk to Rod, but then she relaxed, allowing herself to sink into him. He looked down and smiled at her in approval.

"Rod checks in on the place when I'm not around. I was just getting the lowdown on the lake. The water's been pretty low this year, but last month's rain has got it back up to boating levels. Rod's got a patio boat he lets me use when I'm here."

"Where is here?"

"Lake Shasta. About thirty minutes north of Redding."

"I-I didn't realize you had a place here."

"It's something I bought a few years back."

"Oh." Her implication was clear from her tone. They

hadn't talked enough in the last few years for her to know much of anything about him. But she was surprised Max hadn't said anything about it.

"Do you own it with Max?"

Rhys tensed for a moment. "Nope. This is something that I did completely on my own. Max has come up a few times, but he gets a little antsy when he's here. He's not much for roughing it."

"Somehow I can't see you roughing it much either."

Rod chuckled. "She's got your number, Rhys. But he docs surprisingly well while he's here. He's got some good survival skills, not that you'll be needing them much. Rhys's house is great. It just took him awhile to get it in habitable shape."

Rhys remodeled a house? He obviously had more skill with his hands than she'd thought. Flushing at her thoughts, she blurted, "Is there a restroom here I can use?"

"Use the one in the restaurant. It's nicer than the open restroom by the lake."

She nodded. "Thank you." She rushed into the building, acutely aware of the men's gazes on her. She walked through a little store on the way to the restaurant bathroom, noting the souvenirs and water products for sale. When she was done, she retraced her steps, stopping when a rack of bathing suits caught her eye. Biting her lip, she stared at a white halter-top bikini that was prominently displayed.

If they were going to be staying here a few days and Rhys wanted to go swimming, she'd need something, wouldn't she? She could just see him trying to persuade her to go skinny-dipping, and she wasn't sure she could actually go through with that. Still…

She flipped through the suits on the rack. There were several one-pieces that looked just like the one she had at home. Modest. Flattering. But her eyes kept straying to the white two-piece. She'd never had the guts to wear a bikini before, but hadn't Rhys said being unpredictable was sexy? Maybe this was her chance to prove what a good student she was. Before she could change her mind, she picked it up.

"Would you like to keep the hanger?" the cheerful teenager behind the register asked.

"Um. No, thanks." She handed the girl two twenty-dollar bills.

"I love this suit. I wore it in black just the other day."

Melina briefly closed her eyes. Of course the girl would wear a bikini. She was tall, slim, and had the curves to fill out the swimsuit the way it was meant to be. Melina tried to picture herself wearing the bikini while standing next to this girl's similarly dressed form. Her stomach clenched in horror.

Her hand whipped out to grab the bikini back just as the girl held it out. "Here you go. Have a great day."

Melina stared at the skimpy swatches of fabric, no longer sure the bottom half would cover all that needed to be covered. "You know, I didn't know you had this in black. I think I should wait until you get that in."

The girl frowned. "Oh. I'm sorry, but the bathing

suits aren't returnable."

"Sure. But I just bought it," Melina explained with a bright smile. "It's not like I went out and wore it."

"Well—"

"How about I just exchange it then?" She grabbed a black one-piece from the rack. "This'll do for now. And, look, it's on sale, right?"

"Well, yeah, but—"

"Then I'll take it. You can even keep the difference."

The girl looked nervously at the door that led outside. "I don't know. I guess I could talk to Rod. Explain you changed your mind. Why don't I go out and—"

"No!" Melina yelled in a panic, causing the girl to jerk. "I mean, I don't want to be a bother. I guess I'll take the white bikini after all." She stuffed the thing in her purse and headed for the door. "Thanks," she called. Before she could change her mind, she rushed back to where Rhys and Rod were still talking.

What had she been thinking? She'd never worn a bikini in her life, let alone a white one. She couldn't even wear white pants without it looking like her hips had expanded by several inches. The one-piece would have been safer. But, she reminded herself, that would also have been so predictable of her. Give yourself some props for bravery, she urged herself.

"Your store and restaurant are very nice," she said a bit breathlessly to Rod. "We'll definitely have to come back sometime."

"I'd like that." Rod beamed at them. Inside, Melina

was aghast. Had she just implied that she and Rhys would be back sometime in the future? Together? As in a regular couple? She opened her mouth to correct her mistake, but Rhys put an arm around her shoulders and squeezed. Once more, his expression radiated approval, which confused her even as it made her heart fill with joy.

"It was a pleasure meeting you, Melina. You take care of your man here, you hear?"

Her gaze still on Rhys, she saw the flush stain his cheeks. The thought that he might be a little thrown by what was happening between them calmed her nerves. Take care of Rhys? That was exactly what she was here to do, wasn't it?

So what if she'd never worn a white bikini? Who cared if she never wore the one she'd just bought? She could pretend she was the type of woman who would wear it, right? Doing just that, she lowered her lids and tried to put her breathlessness to work. "Oh, I definitely will take care of him," she murmured.

Both Rod and Rhys looked poleaxed, and an enticing ripple of power thrummed through her. Suppressing a smile, she turned and walked back to the car, putting a little extra swing into her hips. When she glanced back, Rhys's eyes were planted firmly on her behind.

Rhys had failed to tell her one thing about thumbing one's nose at the tried-and-true. It was as much a turn-on to the seducer as it was to the person being seduced.

She climbed into the car and patted her large purse. She'd almost panicked back there, but buying the stupid bikini had changed her. It was like a sexy little secret that only she knew about. Even if all she did was *act* like the type of woman who could wear the thing, no one would be the wiser. And it would be worth it to see that look on Rhys's face again, a combination of surprise and approval, mixed in with a whole lot of desire.

When Rhys got back behind the wheel, he smiled. "Ready to go?"

She placed her hand high on his thigh and squeezed.

He gasped, stared at her hand, and then looked up at her. She kept her eyes wide and innocent. "I'm ready for anything. The question is, are you?"

With a deep breath and a slightly dazed expression, he started the car and pulled back onto the road. Melina leaned back in her seat and smiled. No one could ever accuse her of being anything other than a fast learner.

* * *

Rhys was so aroused by the gentle pressure of Melina's hand on his thigh that he was afraid he was going to pass out. As he pulled up to the property, however, his nerves somehow managed to overshadow his lust.

He tried telling himself he was being ridiculous. He'd never brought a woman here, true, but it wasn't like he was trying to impress Melina with the house. There was nothing grand about it. It wasn't even on the lake, although the water was just a few short minutes' drive away. The house was pre-manufactured, but it had been in such sorry shape that Rhys had had to rebuild about a third of it. Given his touring schedule, he didn't have all that much time to devote to it, but when he did, he worked with utter devotion. He loved puttering around this place. It was as much of a home base as he'd had since he was a kid. He just didn't get here nearly often enough. And while he sometimes called on Max or Rod to help him out with a job or two, for the most part he enjoyed being by himself.

Today, however, he'd felt compelled to show it to Melina. Like it or not, he was nervous to see what her reaction would be.

He needn't have worried.

"Oh, Rhys," she breathed when she caught sight of the little house on an elevated lot at the end of a dirt driveway. "It's wonderful." She got out of the car and turned slowly in a circle, taking in the view of redwood trees and hills. "What a beautiful setting."

He could tell she loved it. The wonder on her face was genuine and closely mirrored the way he'd felt when he'd first seen the land. "Thanks. I like it."

"How did you find it?"

"Rod and I have been friends for a while, ever since Max and I rented a houseboat on the lake years ago. I mentioned that I wouldn't mind having some vacation property up here, and he gave me a call when this lot became available."

She smiled, a broad, carefree smile that made his breath catch. "Will you show me around?"

He laughed. "There's not much to see, but sure, I'll give you the grand tour."

About thirty minutes later, he rubbed his palms together. "So let's go for a picnic by the lake. Take a swim."

She frowned. "But what will I do for a swimsuit?"

A grin split his face. He'd liked the underwear she'd worn last night. He was hoping she had on another set just like it. "I think we can come up with something."

She hesitated, then lifted her chin. "Okay. That would be nice." She moved toward the guest bedroom, stopping when Rhys called out.

"We'll be sharing the bed in the master bedroom, Melina."

She blinked and blushed. Her eyes darted nervously to the open doorway, where his big bed was clearly visible. "Oh. Sure." Changing course, she stepped into the master bedroom and shut the door.

When the bedroom door opened, Melina came out wearing baggy sweat shorts and an oversized tee. Although the clothes did nothing for her figure, Rhys didn't sweat it. Even if he couldn't talk her out of her clothes, water did wondrous things to a white tee.

"I'm ready," she said softly, sounding far less sure of herself than she had when she'd placed her hand on his thigh. Once he'd gotten over the shock, he'd recognized the satisfaction his response had given her. Melina definitely liked a challenge, and he was about to give her the biggest one so far.

"Great. I'll be right back." He went into the bedroom and swiftly changed into shorts and an open button-down shirt.

When he walked out of the bedroom, Melina smiled and turned toward the front door. "Wait," he called. "There's something I need to do first."

"What's that?"

He gently clasped her arms and she tilted her head back, her eyes wide, her lips parting slightly. "I need to give you your first pop quiz."

7

Dalton's Magic Rule #8:
Encourage active participation.

The idea of a pop quiz obviously wasn't something that turned Melina on. She pulled away from him and crossed her arms over her chest, her eyes immediately reflecting her discomfort. "I'm not really big on pop quizzes."

Amusement tipped up one corner of his mouth. No, she wouldn't be. Melina liked to prepare. Research. Have the answers in hand so she could control the situation. Lucky for her, he was here to nudge her out of her comfort zone. "There's no wrong answer to the question I'm about to ask."

She narrowed her eyes suspiciously. "Then it's not really a pop quiz. A quiz implies by its very nature that there's a right answer or a wrong answer."

A huge grin split his face now. "What about multiple-choice questions? Haven't you ever answered a question with D, all of the above?"

"Well, sure," she began hesitantly. "But—"

"There is no 'but,'" he said softly. "Not in this scenario."

Looking like she wanted to argue some more, she simple shrugged and said, "Fine. There are no wrong answers."

"Good. The other thing about this question is that you don't answer it right away. You just think about it. And you answer when you're ready."

"So what's the question?"

"What would you do to have me?"

She stared at him blankly. "Excuse me?"

Reaching out, he rubbed his thumb against her bottom lip, loving the way her eyelids suddenly grew heavy. "That's the question for you to think about. What would you do to have me? Sexually, of course."

Her brows furrowed. "I'm not sure I understand the question. In the context of our…our agreement, I suppose I'll do whatever you tell me pleases you."

"So that's how you plan on handling the next man in your life? Letting him have carte blanche? Anything goes?"

"Well…"

"Bondage?"

Her eyes rounded. "I guess it depends…"

"Sex toys?"

She glanced away, blushing to the roots of her hair. "I-I don't have a problem with—"

"How about multiple partners? Two women? Two men?"

Her eyes snapped back to his. "No. I'm not having any luck keeping one partner satisfied. I don't need an extra person in my bed to worry about."

"How do you know that's your stopping point? Have you ever tried it?"

"No. I've never tried eating worms, either, but I know that's never going to happen."

"Okay, so you have a definite sense of what you wouldn't do. Not so much of what you would."

"Why don't you just tell me what you want, and I'll let you know if it's something I'm not comfortable with."

His expression grew serious. "And is that where your willingness to learn ends? With the obvious answer?"

She reacted just as he expected she would. Challenge Melina's thirst for knowledge and complexity, and expect her to sit quietly and take it? No way. Hands on hips, she thrust her chin out. "Just what are you getting at, Rhys?"

"You know as well as I do that sometimes the key to learning is figuring things out for yourself. Why wouldn't that apply in this situation, as well?"

She came very close to pouting. "Seems to me this is a trick question."

He laughed. "It can't be, because the answer is what it is. If you're willing to do what I ask and nothing more, then that's the answer."

"You're talking in circles," she cried. "I don't want to guess what I need to do. I want to know. That's the whole reason I asked Max for help. I don't want to play the game just to fail again."

His heart skipped as he saw the real distress in her eyes. "Baby, you're not going to fail. There's no way that's possible."

She just shook her head, biting her lip until he wanted to take her in his arms and hold her close. So that's what he did. He pulled her in for a hug and rocked her. She let him hug her but didn't return the favor. Soon, she pulled away.

"I'm sorry. I obviously can't even do this right. I think I should just leave."

"Is that what you really want?" he asked quietly to mask his own desperation. "To quit before we even get started?"

"No. But I don't understand why you're making this so complicated."

"Because despite what you obviously think, men are complicated. Pleasure is complicated. It's not just a matter of telling someone what I like. It's about you figuring it out. Reading the signs. Learning to trust your instincts. And then acting even though it makes you uncomfortable. Because you know that in the end, the pleasure's going to be worth it."

She looked unconvinced. Hell, she practically rolled her eyes, which sure told him something about the degree of pleasure her lovers had been giving her. She was obviously going to need more convincing before she'd willingly agree to his lesson plan.

"Okay, so let's go back to our conversation in the car. You said men wanted overt. An arrow painted with red lipstick falls into that category, right?"

She frowned, obviously not happy with thinking about that little message again.

"Well, things aren't always so black and white—even when the shade is Shanghai Crimson. When you say men like the overt, you're oversimplifying."

"Really. And how's that?"

"What that woman did…it wasn't a turn-on because she sat down across from me practically naked—"

She snorted and he paused, glaring at her.

"Sorry," she muttered.

"It was a turn-on because she went for it. Whatever her reasons, she wanted to have sex with me that much. Not me, necessarily. I could have been Max or any other successful magician, but she was going to get what she desperately wanted, one way or another. Have you ever wanted anything like that, Melina? Because, believe me, I have. And I never thought I had a chance in hell of getting it. Not until I walked into my hotel room last night and found you waiting for me. Not until I realized I'd do anything—run down the Vegas strip naked with lipstick all over my body—to have just one taste of you before you came to your senses and left."

She was breathing hard, her eyes wide and dazed, staring at him as if she'd never seen him before. And she hadn't. Not really. He'd never let her see the passion he harbored for her, not so clear and out in the open. But he was letting her see it now, if she bothered to look.

"Have you ever felt that way about any of your lovers, Melina?"

Slowly, she shook her head.

"Then if your exes found you wanting, it wasn't because you lacked skill. It was because they *knew* you didn't feel that passion for them. That doesn't mean you don't have the passion inside you." I should know, he thought. She'd given him the taste he'd been craving, and it had almost blown his mind.

She shook her head, and her eyes cleared and narrowed. "I don't believe you," she murmured. "What's that old saying? All cats look alike in the dark? A woman without inhibition, a woman who cares only about her own pleasure, makes demands. Her focus isn't on the man. Sure, it's an ego boost to have a woman crazy for him, but in the end the man's going to want his. I'm not the most passionate person, but if I have the skill, that's what's going to matter most."

"I didn't say the woman would only care about her own pleasure the whole time. Great sex is about making a connection, even if it's just on a purely chemical level. It's about give-and-take. It's about someone wanting you for everything you are and aren't, regardless of measurements, wealth, or background. Which is why that woman's forwardness turned me on, but only to a point. She didn't want *me*. She wanted my stage persona. Who she thought I was."

Their gazes locked before she took a deep breath.

"But what you're talking about…it almost sounds like you're describing emotion. Love."

He shrugged, wanting to push the conversation in that direction but knowing that would just scare her. And him, too. He was fortunate to have this weekend. He couldn't get carried away and expect more. "It does, doesn't it? As I said, it's not black and white. Very few things are. This weekend is about experimenting. Learning each other's likes and dislikes. Playing and petting. But it's also about pushing each other to our limits. Finding out what drives us. How far you'll go to have me. That's how you'll learn what pleases a man, Melina. Not by me showing or telling you. By being motivated to figure it out on your own."

"And you think you can motivate me?"

Saying nothing, he shot her a wicked grin. That's all it took to have her blushing. To her credit, however, she didn't go down without a fight.

"So let me get this right. You're saying that instead of giving me clear instructions as to what a man likes, you're going to make me figure it out on my own?"

"I promise to give you lots of feedback. But what I like might not be what another man does. Doing it this way strengthens not only your confidence, but your instincts, too."

"Or it just makes me look like a fool again. And probably leads to a lot of frustration for you."

"If you're willing to take the chance, I think I'll be able to stand it."

She pursed her lips, thinking about it. "I don't know,

Rhys. Maybe this just isn't—"

"What do you say we compromise?"

She took a step back, clearly not trusting him. "How?"

"I'll agree to tell you what I like. What most men like. But each time I do, you need to try something on your own."

"And what if I do something you don't like?"

"Then you win and you won't have to do it again."

"You're that sure of your theory?"

"I'm that sure of you. You can stand there and do nothing and I'll be turned on. You actually do something, anything, to me?" He growled, making her eyes widen.

"In all fairness, how would you know if you win?"

"It's a win-win situation for me, isn't it? I tell you what pleases me, you do it. You try something I like, it pleases me. You try something I don't like, we're back to me telling you what I like. Right?"

She squinted, as if trying to make sense of his convoluted reasoning. "I guess."

"Good. Now, we should probably get going if we want to get in the water before it's cold." He handed her a basket with a blanket and paper goods. "What do you say we play a game on the drive there?"

"A game?"

"Yes. That's something most guys like, too. Teasing. Playing with their partner. Not just physically either. Last night, I pushed you a little to talk to me. To tell me what you like. You ever play the alphabet game?"

She followed him out to the car. "I'm familiar with it."

"Good. Then let's start with that. I was going to propose we start in alphabetical order. Food first. Then the lake. But then I realized I've never really heard you talk dirty before." At the car, he opened the driver's side door and turned to her with one raised brow. "So what do you think, Melina? Can you talk dirty to me? Tell me some of your favorite sex words. And just for kicks, why don't you alphabetize them for me?"

* * *

Melina didn't know why, but something about Rhys's request rankled her.

She got into the passenger seat and slammed the door shut. As Rhys started the engine and pulled out of the driveway, she glared at him. "You don't think I'll do it, do you?"

"Why would I think that? You're very good at following instructions."

She felt her temper spike, still not sure why she was so riled. All she knew was that he seemed too calm and controlled for her liking, especially since she felt anything but. "Meaning what? You don't think I have the creativity to be a good lover? Well, you're right. I don't. But if there's one thing I'm good at, it's words."

"Why are you mad?"

She stared out the windshield and crossed her arms

over her chest. "I-I don't know. Maybe because this seems to be one big joke to you."

He braked so suddenly that she jerked forward against her seat belt. Bracing one hand on the wheel and the other on the headrest behind her, he glared at her. "Tell me one thing I've done to make you think this is a joke to me."

"It's obvious, isn't it? You're trying to make me uncomfortable by drawing things out. Poking fun at my intellectual side."

"I'm not poking fun. I love your intellectual side. Would you rather we just strip and do it a few times to get the nerves out?"

"Yes," she snapped.

"Well, that's not what you need, and it's not what you're going to get from me. If you don't like my methods, I can drive you back home. I'm sure you can get Max to meet you with one phone call."

With that, he shifted in his seat until he again faced forward.

She pressed her lips together, trying not to cry. "I'm sorry. I don't know what's wrong with me. And I don't want to call Max." I want you, she thought. *It's always been you.*

He sighed and started driving again. "There's nothing wrong with you. You're just feeling out of your element. But at some point, for us to go forward, you're going to need to trust me. Trust that I want only the best for you."

She laughed humorously. "So it's my sweet sixteen all over again. You call the shots, and I just wait for you to make your move. Is Trisha James going to make a surprise appearance, too?"

His jaw tightened. "If you want to discuss that night, we can. Frankly, I don't think you're ready to hear what I have to say."

No doubt about it, his words spiked her curiosity. What could he say besides he was sorry? She bowed her head. "No, let's not go there. And I do trust you, Rhys. With this, with me, I trust you."

He said nothing. The mood in the car had grown so serious, and she had only herself to blame. Her one chance to be with Rhys, and what had she done? She'd blown it, all because he hadn't thrown her on the bed as soon as they'd walked into his cabin. Thinking fast, she blurted out, "Afterglow."

"Excuse me?"

"That's my first word. In alphabetical order. Afterglow."

He turned toward her, his mouth tilted up and amusement crinkling the corners of his eyes. "Nice, but a little ahead of yourself, don't you think?"

She breathed a sigh of relief. Maybe she could salvage things, after all. "Blow job," she said, trying to shock him.

"Ah. A personal favorite of mine." He nodded. "But rather predictable."

She uncrossed her arms and shifted closer toward him. She swayed slightly with the gentle vibrations of the car, and placed a hand on the dash to steady herself.

"Clitoris. Co-Cock."

He laughed when she stuttered, but the laugh sounded slightly stilted, so she didn't take offense. "Again, some definite favorites. Keep going."

She wondered if he'd turned on the heater, or if it was just her desire causing her to flush and feel all loose and tingly inside. "Climax. Coitus. Come."

"Wow. Who knew there were so many dirty words that started with C?"

Despite his continued efforts to sound unaffected, she could tell she was getting to him. Sweat had popped out on his upper lip, and his fingers seemed to grip the steering wheel for dear life. His knuckles whitened as she continued.

"Copulate. Cream."

"That's not a dirty word."

"It is if you're licking it off someone's body."

He scowled. "Done that often, have you?"

The idea that he might be jealous had her twisting the truth just a bit. She'd watched a movie recently where whipped cream had been a prominent prop. "Just once. But it definitely showed me what I've been missing."

He didn't respond other than to take a deep breath.

"And now for my personal favorite." Leaning forward, she brushed his ear with her lips and breathed her next word. "Cunnilingus."

He hissed in a breath. When she reached out to put her hand on his thigh again, his hand whipped out, grabbing her wrist. "Don't," he croaked out, his voice guttural.

"Or what?" she whispered.

"Or we're never going to make it into the water. And I for one can use some cooling down." He stopped the car, and she looked around. They'd reached the lake.

"Darn. I was just getting started. But I guess you're right. Guys *do* like dirty talk." She dropped her gaze to his erection, which was straining against the front of his shorts. "At least you do. You sure you don't want to hear the next one?"

He narrowed his eyes at her. "It feels good, doesn't it?"

She drew back, and he slowly released her. "What?"

"Knowing you can get me hard just by talking to me. Knowing that just the sound of your voice pleases me."

"It really does, doesn't it?" she asked, a feeling of wonder making her grin.

"Rein yourself in there, Ladybug. There's only so much a guy can take before he cracks."

"What's your cracking point?" she pouted.

"That's for me to know and—"

"—me to find out."

He winked, then threw open his car door. "Come on. I've worked up an appetite." Grabbing the basket with the blanket, he walked to a shaded spot by the lake. She was still reeling with satisfaction while she unpacked their food. That feeling went out the window five minutes later when Rhys stripped off his shirt. Smooth, tanned skin, defined muscles, and a rippling six-pack nearly mesmerized her.

"What do you want first?" he asked, gesturing to the spread of crusty bread, Gouda cheese, grapes, and prosciutto.

"Uh..." She shook her head. "I'm not that hungry, actually."

"I'll be quick." He reached for a grape. Before she knew what she was doing, she laid her hand over his, stopping him. She was breathing rapidly, her heart hammering in her ears, as she met his gaze. "It's my turn, right? To do what I think will please you?"

His green eyes darkened. "What do you have in mind?"

"Would you...would you lean closer?"

Obediently, he did. She took hold of one plump grape, and lifted it. When he opened his mouth, she placed the grape on his tongue. He chewed the juicy fruit slowly, then swallowed. "Do you...do you want another one?"

"Please."

She took another grape and fed it to him. This time, before he let her draw away, he sucked just her fingertips into his mouth. She inhaled swiftly. Bit by bit, she fed him. The grapes. The bread and cheese. By the time she wrapped a thin piece of prosciutto around her index finger and offered it to him, his breathing was as labored as hers. Taking a gentle hold of her wrist, he guided her finger into his mouth, easing the delicacy off her finger and then sucking the digit strongly.

She moaned. He moaned. After releasing her finger with a pop, he staggered to his feet.

"Rhys," she whispered.

"You're one dangerous lady. I've got to get in the water or I'm going to be all over you."

"So you liked me feeding you?"

"What do you think?"

She swallowed hard. "You liked it."

"Yeah. That's an understatement." And with that, he backed away from her, eyes locked with hers until the last possible moment, then he turned and cannonballed into the water, splashing her with a huge wave that made her yelp even as she laughed out loud.

* * *

"Come on in. The water's great."

Melina stood uncertainly at the edge of the water as Rhys motioned her closer. She wanted close. Closer. She wanted it until her teeth ached. Her body was on fire, and she wasn't sure how much more teasing she could take. There was only one problem.

She was a coward.

She'd been too much of a coward to wear the bikini, and she was too much of a coward to strip down to her bra and panties. Not white, but a pale peach that was so sheer it left nothing to the imagination.

Maybe she squirmed at the thought, because now Rhys was staring at her oddly. She needed to get in that water and fast. What other choice did she have?

"I've already seen everything there is to see, remember?" he asked gently.

Not everything, she thought hysterically. He'd never seen her trying to be the femme fatale. He'd never seen her naked body in full sunlight, every ripple and extra pound of flesh visible. Last night had been different. Last night had been in the dark. Last night, she hadn't known it was him and she'd been buzzed. Why hadn't he brought any wine to go with that romantic picnic?

She jolted when she realized she'd spoken the question out loud.

"Because we're going to take full responsibility for what we're doing. No hiding behind misunderstandings, fuzzy vision, or inebriation. The next time I get between your legs, Melina, you're going to know full well who's there."

"I-I—"

He cocked an eyebrow at her inability to form a comeback.

That made her mad again. Death by frustration, she vowed. He'd be well acquainted with the term before she was through with him.

Taking a deep breath and raising her chin defiantly, she pulled her tee over her head. She heard Rhys's sharp inhalation for breath immediately. Before she could change her mind, she shoved down her shorts, kicked them off, and prepared to dive into the water.

"Stop."

She froze at the intense command in his voice that was accompanied by distinct splashing sounds. He was coming out of the water fast, his hand raised to echo his command. His gaze was riveted on her scantily clad body, the dark heat of it burning her in the best way possible.

He stopped a few feet away from her, water dripping from his hair and shoulders in sinuous streaks that she longed to lap up. All thoughts of teasing him into a frenzy vanished. She stumbled forward, wanting only to fall to her knees, drag his sodden suit down, and take him in her mouth. Instead, she said the first thing that popped into her head. "I bought a bikini at Holiday Harbor, but I'm not the bikini type so I thought I'd just—"

He snorted and moved toward her until he was right in front of her. "You are so the bikini type, Melina." Gently grasping her wrists, he uncrossed her arms and held them out wide. The sheer appreciation on his face made her thighs clench with need. "But I love your lingerie. God, your skin looks so soft. Like cream. And your breasts..." He groaned.

She glanced down at her chest, where her breasts were cupped and lifted by her demi-bra. Her curves were average in size, but her nipples were hard and visibly straining beneath the fabric. Dropping her wrists, he reached out, cupped her breasts in both hands, then pinched her nipples between his fingers, rolling them gently before releasing her.

"Rhys," she whimpered as he dipped his head, suckling first one nipple and then the other. He sucked them hard, as if he wanted to swallow her whole, and she tangled her fingers in his hair, ready to offer her entire self to him. With a groan, he moved to kiss her cleavage, nipping at her skin in a way she knew would leave her bruised. Marked in the best way possible. But then he was backing away from her. Again.

No, no, no.

"The only thing that would be more beautiful than you like this is you like this and wet. Emphasis on the wet part."

Before she could respond, he turned and jumped back in the water.

"You coming in?" His question sounded strangled. As if he'd had to force the words out.

Despite the frustrating ache that he'd caused to buzz through her body again, she smiled. The ache was so much better than the nerves had been. Plus, she was starting to see what Rhys meant about unpredictability and sex being fun even when you were just playing at it. Granted, he had more experience, but that just gave her more to work with.

With a quick movement, she dived in after him.

* * *

Under the relative safety of the water, Rhys cupped his straining dick through his swim shorts. Frantically, he tried to think of something, anything, that would give him a modicum of control as he watched Melina start a lazy crawl toward him. Unfortunately, even thinking of his favorite *Seinfeld* episode couldn't prompt the shrinkage that had caused George Costanza such embarrassment. He was primed and ready to go, especially after her creative alphabetizing and the feel of her fingers feeding him, her eyes transfixed on his mouth the whole time. Seeing her in her sheer bra and underwear had almost driven him over the edge. So what the hell was he waiting for?

When Melina squealed and giggled, then dived under the water to see what had brushed against her, he thought, *This*.

He was waiting for this. Hell, yes, he wanted to enjoy her body, but he wanted so much more than that. The opportunity to play with her. Learn about her. Enjoy her. Once this weekend was over, he'd lose that chance. Melina was letting her guard down because she had an excuse, but once that excuse was gone, the awkwardness and shyness and differences would be back on her radar. In fact, they'd probably be worse.

He'd be Rhys, Max's brother, again. But he'd also be the guy who'd seen her vulnerable and, once she was back in her real world, Melina would remember that.

He had to pack a lifetime of loving Melina in two short days.

When she came back up for air, she was grinning. "You should've warned me we had company."

He shrugged. "You're a nature girl. Fish. Bugs. What's the difference?"

She sniffed. "Surely you jest. Insects are higher on

the evolutionary chain than fish, you know."

His eyebrows shot up. "Really?" He knew a few random facts about insects simply because Melina would occasionally throw them into conversation. He'd even done some independent research because learning more about bugs was one pathetic step closer to learning more about Melina. This, however, he'd never heard before.

She floated on her back, closing her eyes, a contented smile on her lips that made him think of the expression she'd worn when she'd said his name and fallen asleep in his arms. "Mmm. Hmm."

He paddled closer, watching the water hover shallowly above her soft, rounded belly and lush thighs. "And what do you base that theory on?" he asked absently, unable to tear his gaze away from her belly button. He wanted to dip his tongue into it and then work his way downward. "Darwin or Genesis?"

She yawned. "Both, actually. But you don't want to hear about that."

Silently, he caught her by the waist and swung her around to face him. With a startled shriek, she wrapped her arms around his neck, and he urged her legs around his waist. Her eyes rounded as his hardness settled into the cradle of her thighs. Unable to help himself, he pressed her body closer to his and leaned his forehead against hers.

"Right now, I want to hear whatever you want to tell me."

She leaned back and her mouth opened, but then she hesitated. They stared at one another, so close he could see the golden flecks in her warm eyes. Cream and syrup, he thought, leaning down to plant a soft kiss on her shoulder. He lingered, kissed her other shoulder, nipped at it, then laved the small sting with his tongue. "You're the most beautiful thing I've ever seen, Ladybug."

She gasped, bit her lip, and blinked her eyes several times. Just as he leaned down to kiss her, she forced out a laugh, shook her head, and pushed away, looking back at him from over her shoulder. "According to creationism, fish were created on day five, insects on day six, along with man and woman. For evolutionists, life originates in primeval oceans. It's one of the few things the two can agree on. Fish first. Insects after."

"Hmm. I'll be sure to remember that little fact. Come here."

He reached for her, but she swam away again, prompting him to growl in frustration. She'd never teased this way with him. Max, yes. He'd watched her and his brother flirt and touch each other with affection while he did nothing but stand apart, wishing things were different. He liked her teasing far more than he'd ever thought possible.

"I find it interesting, you know—the theory that man and insects were created on the same day. Just like men, male insects are quite willing to perform certain mating rituals in order to get what they want from a female."

Eyes narrowing, he got the distinct feeling she was trying to rebuild a wall between them. He swam closer and, sure enough, she paddled backward. What had he done to scare her? Testing her, he treaded water but let himself float imperceptibly closer. "You make it sound so calculated. Women—and I'm assuming female bugs—have their agenda, their needs, too."

"Tell that to the female bedbug. When she lets a male get close to her, it pierces her body cavity with its penis to deposit sperm. Seems pretty calculated to me."

He frowned. "What are you saying, Melina? You're afraid I'm going to hurt you? Male insects don't exactly have it easy, you know. Everyone knows what happens to a male praying mantis when he mates."

Confusion swept over her expression, making her look like the little girl he'd met when her parents had first come to help his parents. Again, she seemed to force out a little laugh. "The female only occasionally bites off his head. Only when it's well deserved, I'm sure." She shook her head, her expression growing somber. "Seriously, of course I don't think you're going to hurt me. I guess what I'm trying to say is that I know how things go. That's why I want to learn all I can about physically pleasing a man. The flowers. Chocolates. Deep conversation that a man puts out when he's interested in a woman? It's all part of the mating ritual. A man puts forth great effort to catch a woman's attention so he can get what he wants."

Not liking what he was hearing, he circled her like a shark, noting the increased color in her cheeks and the rapidness of her breaths. "I'm still not getting your point."

"My point is…you don't need to do it. The teasing. The picnic. The compliments." She waved the air separating them. "The little lessons on trust and submission. All this. I don't need to be wooed, Rhys. I'll give you what you want. I'll give you anything you want this weekend."

Her message was implied but clear. This weekend, but not longer. He lunged for her and she squealed, barely managing to elude his grasp this time.

Despite the slow build of anger inside him, he tried grinning wolfishly. "I'm the teacher here, remember, baby? Or have you decided there's a thing or two you can teach me? If so, I'll spread myself out on that picnic blanket right now so you can show me your stuff. You'll get my point loud and clear."

Her eyes widened, and he could see her thinking. What she said, however, nearly blew him out of the water. "What about spreading yourself out on a bed and letting me tie you down? Would that be unpredictable enough for you?"

8

Dalton's Magic Rule #9:
Tie someone up and use a little mood music.

After her bold declaration, Melina heard nothing but the gentle lapping of the water. Unable to stand it, she looked down, straining her eyesight as if she could see one of the fish that had brushed against her. Maybe she'd been too bold? Crossed the line? Hadn't he said they'd play by his methods or not at all?

"Look at me." Shivering at his hoarse command, she reluctantly raised her head. She gasped at the intense desire reflected in his hooded eyes, which blazed at her like ice-hot gems, but she didn't miss the edge of temper surrounding them either. "It depends what's driving you. Are you scared of me? Because if that's it, then this whole thing—"

"I'm not scared," she rushed out. "I told you I trust you, and I do. It's just something I've never done before. All my other lovers, I would've felt silly asking them. But with you—" She shook her head. "Never mind. It was another stupid idea—"

"Come here, Melina."

The way he said it, with more than a hint of a dare, made her heart leap out of control. To counter it, she cocked a brow, but she didn't move any closer to him. "Why?"

In response, he glided slowly toward her until they were treading water next to each other, his legs occasionally bumping against hers. What had he said about seeing her wet? Because if he touched her in the right place—she almost whimpered at the thought—he'd feel she was far wetter than mere water could make her. She was also so hot she was surprised the water around them hadn't started to boil.

Reaching out, he cupped her cheek, soothing his thumb across her brow in a tender gesture that still managed to make her think of that big bed in his bedroom and him tied down and spread out for pleasure. His and hers. He smirked as if he could read her mind. "Because I'm going to kiss you. And then we're going to get out of this lake, pack up my stuff, drive back to my house, hopefully without crashing, and you're going to tie me up. But on one condition."

He floated closer, until her nipples brushed against his chest in a teasing dance choreographed by the water surrounding them. Desire coursed through her, a heavy ache that made her want to wrap her arms around him and sink into the liquid depths below, like a siren whisking her sailor away from his duties in favor of decadent sensation.

Unable to help herself, she reached out and placed her hands on his shoulders, cupping the balls of muscle there even as she reestablished her position with her legs around his waist. "What's that?"

Anticipation, an exhilarating mix of fear and lust, clawed at her. With sure hands, Rhys cupped the cheeks of her bottom and arched into her, indicating loud and clear that playtime was over. He waited until her low moan faded before answering her. "I get to return the favor."

* * *

They didn't crash on the drive back to Rhys's house, but it was touch and go—literally—the entire time. Mainly, she did the touching, teasing Rhys from the passenger seat, her hands smoothing across his chest, stroking his thighs, cupping the spectacular package in between while he gritted his teeth and tried to focus on the road, his white knuckles gripping the steering wheel for dear life. During that wild five-minute ride, she savored the now-familiar intoxicating rush of power, the sure knowledge that *she* was the reason he was barely holding on to his control. The power shifted, however, when she began to kiss him.

She started at his neck, at the corners of his mouth, and was working her way downward when he suddenly braked and tugged her head away. With his ragged breaths filling the small confines of her car, he subdued her attempts to pull away from him, shaking his head warningly. "We're almost there." The rough tenor of his voice slid across her skin like nubby silk, rich and smooth but with enough texture to tease rather than satisfy.

"Then why'd you stop?" she whispered even as she craned her neck in a desperate bid to kiss his lips.

The hand on her hair tightened, and the bite of pleasure-pain made her eyes widen. The deep clench of need between her thighs made it more than clear that she just might like things rougher than she'd ever imagined.

"Because your hands on me are one thing, but if your lips get any closer to my dick, then we're not going to make it to my bed. I'm going to pull over and take you right here, and that's not what you asked for—"

"I changed my mind," she breathed, silently cursing her stupidity. She forgot why she'd ever come up with the idea of tying him down. If he was tied down, he couldn't use his hands on her, and she wanted his hands on her. So much that she was about to beg for it, but he gave a sharp shake of his head.

"Kiss me. One kiss. And then sit back like a good little girl until we get there."

She dug her nails into his shoulders, giving him a taste of the hunger rolling through her. "But I don't want to be a good little girl. Not anymore."

He growled and took the kiss he'd asked for. His lips surrounded hers, his tongue sank deep, and the whole time he kept his hands on her skull, in her hair, guiding her mouth, tilting it this way and that, demanding that she give him what he wanted. Then he pushed her away.

"Don't move," he said as he released her and then turned back to the road, starting to drive with a jerky lurch. It was a hard order to obey, but she dug her fingernails into her palms, consoling herself that they'd be there soon. As she stared at him, however, a devilish urge to push him even closer to the edge took control of her. She'd always been reluctant to talk dirty in bed, but now the urge was driving her hard.

"The first thing I'm going to do when you're tied down is take you in my mouth," she said softly.

He jerked in surprise and looked at her, then clenched his jaw as he focused on the road again.

"I-I haven't had a lot of experience with it," she confessed, "because I've never really liked it. But with you, I want to taste every inch of you. Lock you in my mouth. In my throat, so you can never get away."

He flinched. Groaned. Lowered his hand to cup himself. But just for a second. When he had both hands on the wheel again, he glared at her, the glint in his eyes promising retribution. "And when I'm in your throat and can't get away, what are you going to do?"

"I-I—" She struggled for something clever to say. Something nasty and hot and depraved. But all she could manage was the truth. "I'm going to suck you until you come."

He hissed out a breath and took a sharp turn. "Unless you come first."

"What do you mean?" she asked dumbly.

The car stopped. She barely noticed that they'd made

it back to the house. "I mean I don't just lay back when a woman is pleasuring me with her mouth, Melina. I give it right back to her."

Stunned, she could do no more than gape at him while he rounded the car, pulled open her door, then swept her into his arms, carrying her up the steps into the house with a rushed agility that took her breath away. Maneuvering into his bedroom, he deposited her gently on the bed. He gave her another one of those intense, dominating kisses and started to strip her. Her hands raced to follow his lead, but somehow he managed to get her naked before she could do more than push his shirt from his shoulders.

He pinned her hands next to her head, his cheeks flushed, his breathing rough, and a decidedly dazed look in his eyes. "I can't do it."

She jerked in surprise and shame filled her fast. "What?" This is it, she thought. I was wrong before. *This is where he hurts me.*

"I can't wait. I'm sorry, Melina, I thought I could but—" He closed his eyes and leaned his forehead against hers, just as he had at the lake. With his touch, she realized he was shaking. "If I can't have you now, I think I'm going to die."

His blatant honesty stunned her. He was as wet as she, their hair damp, his trunks hiked up the muscled thigh that pressed between her legs so that her bare flesh met his. Instead of being embarrassed by the wetness there, as she normally would have been, she reveled in it. Instinctively, she pressed herself toward him, wanting more pressure on the tiny bundle of nerves that was swelling for his touch. It wasn't close enough, so she struggled to get her hands free. When he wouldn't release her wrists, she leaned up and kissed him gently, then followed the tender touch with a nip to his bottom lip. "It's okay, Rhys. I don't want to wait either."

"But you said you wanted to play—"

"Playing can wait." She swallowed and forced herself to say it. "I've wanted you for so long. On top of me. Inside me. If that's what you want—"

He took one of her hands and slid it inside his trunks, covering her fingers with his until she was grasping him tightly. Moving her hand, he started a smooth, steady friction that made his eyes close and his head fall back. "I want."

"Then take me," she whispered.

With a rough groan, he stood, pushed down his swimsuit, and lunged for the bedside table where he removed a small square packet. Ripping it open, he slipped the condom over himself and then came on top of her. She welcomed him, arms and thighs opened wide, and he sank onto her.

Sinking into her wasn't quite as easy.

He pushed the head of his penis against her, groaning as her tight muscles slowly allowed him inside. Inch by inch he took her, eyes open now, staring into her soul and refusing to let her look away. When he gave a final heavy push, sinking into her all the way, her mewl of pleasure mixed melodically with his deep-throated groan.

Immediately, he started a shallow thrusting that steadily increased in speed and impact.

"Rhys?" she gasped when he hit a spot inside her she'd never known existed. Apparently, Rhys didn't need any help finding her G-spot.

He kissed her lightly, a teasing brush of his lips that had her arching to get closer to him. "You feel so good. Just as I've always imagined."

The idea that he might have imagined this before brought tears to her eyes. She gripped his shoulders tighter even as her internal muscles clenched around the thick rod inside her. The drag of his cock against her sensitive nerves pushed her so high so fast it left her stunned. She marveled at this man's ability to destroy her at the same time he renewed, replenished, and recharged her. "I'm going to come, Rhys," she wailed, not wanting to leave him behind again.

His thrusts came even faster now. "Come, baby. I'll be right there with you."

And he was. Together, they groaned and shuddered, muscles tightening and clenching, breath heaving, fingers grasping as they took each other over the edge. And just like before, when she came down from the pinnacle, she was in Rhys's arms, shivering and whispering his name. This time, however, her mind didn't form her favorite fantasy.

It didn't have to.

Her fantasy was in her arms, pushing back her hair and whispering the sweetest words she'd ever thought to hear. Feeling her heart expanding with love for him, she tried to pull back. To protect herself while she still could.

"So does this count as something you told me you liked?" she gasped, taking a deep breath before she could continue. "Or something I came up with on my own?"

"I don't know and I don't care," he whispered. "All I know is I want to do it again. And again—" He kissed her ear and worked his way down to her shoulder, continuing the kisses as he repeated the words over and over. "And again."

* * *

For the rest of the evening, "again" and "more" became Rhys's personal mantra. Melina engraved the words in her memory, cherishing them but also taking them as a challenge. Part of her never wanted him to stop saying those words, so she pushed herself to do things she'd never been comfortable with.

First, remembering a scene from *Sex and the City*, she straddled him. With her back arched and her hands raised above her head, she rode him so fast and so hard that her breasts bounced. Well, not quite. Samantha's breasts had bounced on the show. In real life, Melina's breasts just jiggled. Still, given Rhys's response, jiggling definitely worked for him.

Next, she resumed their alphabet game, breathing out a new word in time to his deep, languid strokes, and eventually cursing him when he refused to let her orgasm until she finished. He laughed and pressed her hips down, controlling her movements, and she almost panicked when she got to "X." Somehow, she came up with "xenerotica," the act of getting turned on by strangers. Then, when she got to "Z," he reached down and touched her where they were joined. She came apart, screaming "zelophilia" so loud she barely heard his own groans of pleasure. He collapsed next to her, struggling for breath.

"Zelophilia?" he asked skeptically.

"Sexual arousal from jealousy," she breathed back.

"How "

Turning on her side, she rested her head on his shoulder and closed her eyes, smoothing her fingers over his muscular chest. "My friend Lucy is a Scrabble fanatic."

They took a break for dinner, munching on more of the savories that Rhys had packed for lunch before he started a fire. Now they sat on the couch, Melina practically in his lap and Rhys playing with her hair. Enveloped in a soft blanket, she stared at the fire, wondering what part of the day would become her favorite fantasy once the weekend was over.

"You went somewhere," he said. "What's wrong?"

She jolted, stunned that he would pick up on her change of mood so quickly. Forcing herself to smile, she shook her head. "Nothing. I just realized I never got to tie you up. Or down, for that matter."

His hand stilled. "So what's stopping you?"

She kissed his shoulder. "I'm not sure I have that kind

of energy right now. Can we try tomorrow, maybe?"

Blowing out a beleaguered sigh, he shrugged. When he spoke, his voice was tight. "I can't make any promises about that."

Fear had her heartbeat racing. Pulling away, she sat up, searching his face. "I'm sorry. If you want to, we can do it now. I just thought we could—"

He shook his head and cupped her face in his hands. "I was kidding, Melina."

Closing her eyes in relief, she slapped his shoulder. "I knew that."

"You did, huh?" He pulled her back into his arms so that her back rested against his chest and his chin nudged the top of her head. He took a deep breath. "You still use the shampoo your mom made for you."

"Mmm. I guess I'm just a creature of habit." She peered up at him. "Although you're certainly changing that."

"I haven't changed anything," he said seriously. "You're still the same person you were. You're just giving yourself permission to be who you really are."

"Hmm. Well, one thing's for sure. I never thought I'd get here."

"Here?"

"In your…I mean, one of the Dalton twins' arms," she clarified in a panic.

Rhys stiffened.

She cringed.

Holy moly. Had she actually said that? Not only did

she almost reveal how she felt about Rhys, but she'd pretty much implied he and Max were interchangeable. Remembering what he'd said about the woman in the trench coat and lipstick wanting him for his stage persona, rather than himself, she shook her head and wrenched around to face him. "I mean—"

Rhys released her and stood. The frown on his face confirmed that he'd taken her words in the worst way possible.

"So were you thinking of me or Max the whole time?" he said.

"Rhys, I'm sorry. That's not—"

"Maybe you switched back and forth depending on what we were doing? Tell me, was it me you were riding like a wild bronco, or was it my brother?"

She stood, pulling the blanket around her when his hard gaze swept down her naked body. For the first time, she saw disgust in his eyes. She reached out, cringing when he pulled away. "That's not what I meant, Rhys. Honest. Please don't think that."

"I don't know why I'm surprised," he said. Raking his hands through his hair, he laughed, a bitter, rancorous sound. "You've always preferred Max's company to mine. Hell, you asked *him* for a sexual favor. Was it really because of what your boyfriends said, or had it just been a long time for you? Need an itch scratched? Call Max. And, heck, if he can't do it, there's always Rhys."

Feeling like she was suddenly traversing a minefield, Melina said, "No, that's not—"

Rhys snorted. "No? Come on, Melina, you just said it yourself. Either one of us would have done the trick. Apparently, nothing's changed in twelve years." He turned away, stalking toward his bedroom.

Stunned, Melina stared at his broad back and tight behind, not sure what had just happened. When his reference to that night twelve years ago registered, however, she narrowed her eyes. "You-you big jerk!" she cried.

Rhys froze and slowly turned toward her. "You big jerk?" he taunted. "You pulled out 'xenerotica' and 'zenophilia,' but that's the best thing you can come up with?" He strode toward her, the look on his face making her back up in spite of herself. "Come on, Melina. You can do better than that. You're a master with words, right?"

"Stop," she whispered, torn apart by the nastiness in his tone.

He took hold of her arms then released them, his touch hovering as if he wanted to shake her but was fighting not to. "You used the words 'cock' and 'dick' before. How about 'asshole'? That's always a good one."

"Why are you so angry?" she said. "I know what I said sounded bad, but you know I've always loved you."

"You know what? I don't need that kind of love. At least the women who want to fuck me for my fame are honest about their motives. You had to pull the pity card to get one of us in your bed."

She jerked back, too shocked to form a comeback.

By the look on his face, he'd managed to stun himself.

He reached out for her. "Oh, shit. I'm sorry, Melina. I didn't mean—"

She shoved him away with both hands, managing to knock him back a step. "You...you prick!" Blinded by tears, she whirled and tried to run, but her legs got caught up in the blanket and she tripped, falling to the floor. Stunned more than hurt, she flopped around, trying to free her arms and legs so she could get away.

He crouched down next to her, trying to help her. She slapped his hands away. "Don't touch me," she screamed.

"I'm sorry I said that, Melina. I'm sorry I blew up at all. Will you please listen to me? Please?"

Since he was crowding her and she was shaking so hard that she couldn't get to her feet, she sat up and wrapped her arms around her knees, squeezing them to her chest. In the back of her mind, she remembered she'd started all this with her poor choice of words. Somehow, however, his anger and hostility—something she'd never faced before—wouldn't allow her to soften.

"Fine. But the minute you're done, I'm leaving." She focused her gaze on the corner of the blanket. Idiot, she thought. She'd known if she ever let herself believe in him that things would end badly. And now she had to live the rest of her life knowing exactly what she was missing.

He nodded. "Okay. If that's what you want, I'll drive you back."

"I'll drive myself back," she snapped. "You can figure out how to get to...to wherever you're going next on your own."

"Okay." He held out his hands. "Okay, fine." Slowly, he lowered himself to the floor, sitting in front of her. He dipped his head, trying to get her to look at him. "First, I apologize for what I said. I swore I'd never deliberately hurt you, and I did. Will you accept my apology?"

Still refusing to look at him, she shrugged, refusing to say more.

"What you said about wanting to be with a Dalton twin, it obviously pressed a big button of mine."

She traced the grain on a plank of hardwood. "I didn't mean it the way it sounded," she said grudgingly.

"Okay, but you can see how I mistook your meaning, can't you? And why it might bother me that you just saw me as a sexual substitute for my brother?"

Forcing herself to look up, she nodded. "Yes. I can see that, and I tried to apologize right away and explain."

"I know you did. I accept your apology. Will you explain now?"

She saw the genuine regret on his face and felt it herself. She hated the idea of hurting Rhys or of him being mad at her, but she couldn't cave either. Not without some sort of explanation. "First, I want to know what you meant about me not having changed in twelve years."

He hesitated briefly. "I meant the way you kissed Max in the gazebo, when I'd asked you to meet me there. I know it was a one-time thing, but I've always viewed that as you exchanging one Dalton twin for the other."

Amazed, she straightened. "And how do you think I felt about Trisha? There I was, waiting for you for over an hour, thinking you were going to finally...and you were making out with her the whole time. I didn't exchange Max for you. He was just trying to make me feel better. That's why he kissed me. And I'm sorry if that bothers you, but given what you'd done, I don't think you have a right to point fingers at anyone."

Rhys shook his head, confusion creasing his forehead. "What do you mean, I was making out with Trisha the whole time? I never made out with her."

Abruptly hiking the blanket to her thighs, Melina jumped to her feet. "Why are you lying?"

Getting to his feet more slowly, Rhys strode past her and into his bedroom.

She watched him in disbelief. "Where are you—"

Before she could finish the question, he was back, pulling on a pair of shorts with stiff, jerky movements. "Did Max tell you I was making out with Trisha?"

She hugged her arms to her chest, not knowing what to think. "Yes. Are you telling me you weren't?"

"That's exactly what I'm telling you."

She pulled the blanket tighter around her. "But why would Max lie?"

"I've got a pretty good idea." Rhys threw his hands up in the air and began pacing. "No wonder he felt so bad afterward. Telling me it was nothing. That he'd initiated it. That I shouldn't let it stop me from telling you how I feel." Coming to a stop, he pointed his finger at her for emphasis. "I sent Max out to tell you why I was late. I caught Trisha throwing up in the bathroom. Caught her *making* herself throw up. You know how obsessed she was with staying thin. Well, she freaked when I caught her. Thought I would tell her parents, and I sat down with her, telling her that's exactly what she should do. When she'd calmed down and finally agreed, I was walking her out when I saw you kissing Max. Then you just left. When I tried to talk to you, you—"

Shaking, Melina lowered herself to the couch. "I froze you out. I was so crushed, I didn't want to talk to you. Never wanted to talk about that night."

Rhys dropped down next to her, his elbows on his knees, staring at the floor between his feet.

"You said you had something you wanted to tell me that night. What was it?"

Rhys pressed his lips together. "I was going to ask you out."

It was what she'd hoped, but to hear him verify it after all these years was almost too good to be true. "Out, out?"

A slow smile curved Rhys's lips. "Yes. Out, out."

"So you liked me, liked me?" Melina knew she sounded like an idiot, but the ways things were going, she wanted things to be crystal clear.

"Yes," Rhys said simply.

"I liked you, too. I still do," she whispered.

Reaching out, he took her hand and squeezed. "Like me, like me?"

She laughed. "Yes."

"Do you still like me enough to give me a hug?"

She practically leaped into his arms, knocking him over so he fell back with her on top of him. Their mouths met for several long, deep kisses before she pulled back. "I want to ask you something," she confessed, "but I'm afraid you'll get mad again."

He hugged her closer. "I might, but I promise to stay calm and let you say what you need to."

Reaching out, she traced his lips with a finger. Teasingly, he caught the tip of her finger in his teeth, making her giggle. Since the topic was obviously so important to him, however, she forced herself to be serious. "Do you really think people view you and Max as interchangeable? Anyone who knows you sees the differences between you."

Smoothing his hands up and down her back, he said, "Yeah? And what differences do you see?"

"Max is less certain of himself, and he disguises it by acting cocky. It's why he sleeps with so many women, and why he jokes around so much. You're more introspective, more serious. You put the weight of the world on your shoulders because you care about people so much. Like what you told me about Trisha. You interrupted your own plans to talk with her. Max wouldn't have. Not that Max doesn't care, but he wouldn't have felt comfortable getting that close to someone's scars. He'd have helped her, but by grabbing one of us or your mother to talk to her."

For a moment, Rhys couldn't respond. He was so choked up by how she saw him that he almost wanted to duck his head and hide for fear that she'd see just how much. Max was more comfortable with people, but she was right: It was mostly on a superficial level. Rhys, their parents, Melina—they were the only ones Max had ever really trusted enough to let inside. Rhys's circle wasn't that much bigger, so he knew Melina was exaggerating to a degree. He still liked how she saw him.

"There's another difference between you, but I'm not sure if I should tell you. It might give you a big head," she whispered.

He grinned and arched his hips into her, making her gasp. "Too late for that."

She stretched up so she could whisper in his ear, deliberately dragging her nipples against his chest. "You promise you won't tell anyone?"

Dropping his hands to her lush hips and pulling her in tighter, Rhys groaned, "I promise."

Raising herself up slightly, Melina looked directly into Rhys's eyes. "You're way better looking than Max," she deadpanned.

Rhys's eyes widened, then narrowed. "You little—" Digging his fingers into Melina's sides, he tickled her, making her screech and laugh with delight even as she struggled to get away.

He ceased tickling her almost immediately and instead wrapped his arms around her, hugging her tight. The last thing he wanted, he realized, was for her to get away.

9

Dalton's Magic Rule #10:
Know when to move on.

The next morning, Melina woke to a curious swishing sound. Stretched out on her stomach and nestled under Rhys's down comforter, she patted the bed next to her, confirming that Rhys was no longer with her. Blinking her eyes open, she yawned and stretched, hissing at the soreness in long-neglected muscles even as she grinned. Rolling slowly onto her back, she stared at the ceiling, straining her ears to identify the sound that continued to drift through the closed bedroom door.

A flash of white caught her eye, and she bolted into a sitting position, then fumbled for her glasses on the nightstand. After jamming them on her face, she stared at the white pieces of fabric slung over the doorknob.

It was the bikini she'd bought. The one she'd taken out of her purse and then chickened out of wearing. She'd stuffed it into her overnight bag before they'd left for the lake, only Rhys had obviously found it. Her first reaction was embarrassment. Sure, he'd said she was a bikini girl, but something this flashy and risqué? Something so out of character for her? Had he been amused by her purchase or turned on?

Standing, she moved toward the door and picked up the bikini, grimacing at the little piece of string that was supposed to (not) cover her bottom. But the longer she looked at it, the more certain she became.

It had turned him on, she decided.

Why wouldn't it? It answered the pop quiz he'd given her. If the bikini didn't prove how far she was willing to go to have him, she wasn't sure what would.

But then she frowned.

She'd bought the bikini, yes, but she hadn't worn it. And, worse, he'd probably guessed why.

Swoosh. Swoosh. The strange sound was a bit louder now that she was so close to the door. Whatever he was doing out there, she tried to imagine his reaction if she sauntered out wearing nothing but the bikini. She got all hot thinking about it, so she quickly pulled on the bottom piece, then looked down at herself. Since she'd waxed, her bikini line was bare. Her skin looked smooth and somewhat creamy, just liked he'd said. Unfortunately, if she looked closely she could see the first sign of stubble on her calves, and she knew from behind she had a dimple or two or ten that she wouldn't be able to hide. Suddenly she wasn't feeling so hot.

She bit her lip, undecided. This was her last day with

Rhys. She wanted to make the most of it. Did she really want to wear something she felt less than confident in?

Shaking her head, she quickly pulled off the bottom, returned the pieces to her overnight bag, and then rushed into the bathroom to brush her teeth and dress. Compromising, she pulled on the shorts and pretty lavender tank top she'd bought for the weekend. It showed more skin than she normally did, so she didn't feel quite as cowardly as she did about the bikini.

She opened the door, then froze, sucking in her breath at the sight in front of her.

Rhys stood in the living room with the front door open. He was wearing jeans but nothing else. Sunlight illuminated his bare chest and muscular arms as he rhythmically worked sandpaper across some kind of wooden frame. A light layer of sweat covered him, and he paused to swipe at his forehead, then downed some water from a bottle. Staring at his throat as he chugged the water, Melina licked her lips and automatically stepped forward, wanting to wrap her arms around him and get all sweaty herself.

He glanced up and saw her, his smile making her knees tremble. He put down the water bottle. "Hey."

"Hey," she said back, moving closer.

His eyes swept down her body. "Very sexy. But it's not a bikini."

His exaggerated pout made her laugh. "No."

"I hope you don't mind that I went through your bag. I threw your shorts and tee into the wash, and figured I'd throw in anything else that needed to be washed, too."

"That was very thoughtful. Thank you."

"You're welcome," he replied, looking amused.

She peered at what he was working on. She'd been right—it was a frame, with gentle curves, scrolled corbels, and intricate beadwork. "Oh, Rhys. What a beautiful mantel."

Grinning, he swiped his hand across the top. "Isn't it? Someone painted it, and I've been wanting to get to the grain underneath. Since you were sleeping, I thought I'd try to get some of it done before we leave."

His voice trailed off and he frowned. Wishfully, she wondered if it was because he didn't like the idea of their weekend ending. Since he didn't say that, she just nodded, trying to tell herself the sudden tightness in her throat was a result of all the talking they'd done last night. Looking around, she grabbed a banana from the counter and backed toward the bedroom. "You can keep working on it. I have some stuff I need to read anyway. I'm presenting at a conference this week…"

Now it was her turn to frown. Hello. Conference. Jamie. Baby.

The day before yesterday she'd been imagining holding Jamie's baby. She hadn't thought of him once since being with Rhys. She certainly hadn't spared a thought, enthusiastic or otherwise, for their after-conference drink date. That was so not good.

Despite Lucy's concerns, Melina genuinely liked Jamie. He was attractive. Kind. Deep. She'd been excited by the prospect of going out with him. By the possibility of their future together. Heck, she'd liked him enough to try to turn herself into a sexual dynamo. In truth, she could barely remember what he looked like. All she saw—all she smelled and felt and longed for—was Rhys. Now here he was in front of her, and all she could think about was how it was going to end.

"Melina? Are you okay?"

She bit her lip, wanting to shout, *No, I am not okay.* She'd never be okay. Not after this. "You know how I am with public speaking," she forced out. "I'm presenting a workshop with Jamie. It's a wonderful opportunity since I'll be just one of three on a panel. Jamie talked me into it, but I guess I'm still more nervous than I'd hoped."

"You'll do great." He put down the sandpaper, walked around the mantel, then held out his arms. "Can I have a morning kiss?"

She walked into his arms, squeezing him tightly and kissing him so eagerly that her teeth scraped against his. Obviously sensing her desperation, he pulled back, his brows furrowed. He smoothed a hand over her hair. "Tell me what's wrong."

"Nothing, nothing." She pulled away and jerked her thumb over her shoulder. "I'm just going to grab my paperwork and read in the bedroom if you don't mind."

"Are you sure?"

"Yes. I really need to catch up."

He looked like he wanted to argue, but simply said, "One hour and then we can go into town. I'll buy you lunch, and we can walk around?" The hesitation in his voice indicated he was thrown off balance by her strange mood, and she struggled to reassure him. The last thing she wanted was him feeling sorry for her when they went their separate ways.

"That sounds perfect." Feeling like her face was going to crack because she was smiling so hard, she backed into the bedroom and gave him a cheery wave. Hesitantly, he waved back.

She shut the door. Leaning her forehead against it, she tried telling herself that the weekend wasn't over yet. She had the whole day with him before he left for...for...

She scrunched up her face.

She didn't even know where he was going when he left her.

With the thought came a wave of intense emotion. Dropping the banana on the floor, she covered her mouth with both hands in order to stifle the grief that tried to pour out of her. Turning, she stumbled, but she didn't even make it to the bed. Slowly, she sank to the floor and curled into a fetal position.

She was splintering apart, she thought. No matter how tightly she squeezed her eyes shut, the tears leaked out, all the more painful for their silence.

* * *

Rhys stared at the closed bedroom door, once more debating whether to follow Melina. He got within two feet of it, his hand raised to knock, before he turned away. Rubbing his hands over his face, he muttered a curse. Several curses.

When he'd mentioned the end of the weekend, he'd thought he'd seen a flash of panic on Melina's face that echoed his own. But then she'd started talking about the conference, and he wasn't sure what to think. All he knew was that he didn't want to leave her. Only, how could he justify that to her or himself?

Everything he'd told Max was still true. They wanted different things in life. If he had only himself to consider, he wouldn't hesitate to make changes. But it wasn't just him. He was an integral part of the Dalton Twins' Magic Show. Plenty of people were counting on him, including his mom and dad, who'd sacrificed their retirement funds to invest in their children's dreams. Their crew and their assistants had families they had to support, and Max... Rhys closed his eyes. Max was smart and he was talented, but he just didn't have the focus or the drive to deal with the business aspects of the act.

So ask her to come with you, he thought.

He glanced at the doorway again. She'd already shown she was far more adventurous than he'd ever believed. Hell, that little bikini he'd found had just about knocked him off his feet. He could easily picture her in it, her perky breasts high and firm, her curvy hips and ass mouthwateringly exposed.

How could he really know what she wanted unless he asked?

For the first time, he allowed himself to feel hope where Melina was concerned.

Turning back to the mantel, Rhys started sanding with vigor.

One hour, he'd told her. He'd finish up, take her out, maybe get her some wine with her lunch, and then he'd ask her what she thought about extending her little experiment.

Indefinitely.

* * *

After walking Shasta's small downtown with its quaint shops, including a gold rush museum, Rhys took Melina to his favorite outdoor bistro. As the waiter delivered their meals, Melina deliberately ignored the beautiful weather, as well as the vibrant bursts of azalea vines and roses that climbed the iron trellis surrounding the patio. Instead, she forced herself to remember the intense pain that had crippled her that morning. She knew that in order to avoid even more pain, she had to get away from Rhys as soon as possible.

"How about some wine?" Rhys asked.

Without glancing up from her salad, Melina shook her head. "Better not. I have a bit of a stomachache."

"What? Why didn't you tell me?"

At the genuine concern in Rhys's voice, Melina looked up. Guilt almost made her wince. He looked so concerned, and for no reason. She'd only said she had a stomachache to prepare for her escape, but she didn't want to ruin their last moments together, either. Reaching out, she squeezed his hand. "It's not too bad, but I should probably just stick with water."

He lifted her hand to his mouth and kissed it. Melina closed her eyes, commanding herself not to cry. "So," she forced out, pulling her hand back. "You've got a show coming up, right? Where will you be performing next?"

"Reno."

Her eyebrows rose. "Reno. Not one of your more exotic locals."

Laughing, he shook his head. "No. But it's definitely one of our most important shows."

"Why's that?"

He leaned back in his seat. "There are going to be some important people watching on Wednesday night. In a way, we'll be auditioning for them. Seven Seas Cruises pulls out of Florida. They want the Dalton Twins' Magic Show to be part of their onboard entertainment, which means we'd have a permanent theater to work out of."

Although she wondered why she hadn't heard anything about this before, even from Max, surprise and excitement rushed through her so intensely that she squealed. Despite his casual demeanor, she could plainly see how much the cruise ship opportunity meant to him. "Oh. My. Gosh!" She jumped up and threw her arms around him. "That's amazing. How wonderful. Your parents must be thrilled. You and Max are hitting the big time, just like you always wanted."

"Yeah. Just like we always wanted."

Something in his voice made her step back. Mixed in with his excitement was something akin to nerves. Even doubt. "Is something wrong?"

He laughed nervously. "Other than the fact I'm sometimes prone to motion sickness? Nah. I've been assured the Seven Seas ships have the best stabilizers in the business."

She moved back to her chair and sat down. "So when does this contract start?"

"We have to get it first, but then it's supposed to start immediately."

She waved her hand, indicating it was practically a done deal. "They'll recognize your talent when they see it," she said brightly. "But what about the rest of your tour?"

"We have one more gig lined up in Vegas, and then we'd planned to take some time off. Our availability is a huge factor in our favor. Their cruises last from seven to twenty-one nights, depending on the itinerary."

"Wow. And you'd be performing every night?"

"That's the plan." He shrugged. "There's one sticking point. They want an act for their family show, too. I'm not sure we can give them that."

"Why not?"

"The act's taken a turn since you last saw it. To compete with others, we've upped the adult nature of our shows."

She'd been about to take a bite of her salad, but her fork froze in front of her face. "Adult nature?" she echoed.

"Nothing vulgar," he said quickly. "Skimpy outfits. Sexual humor." His voice remained steady, but a slight blush had risen on his cheeks.

"Just how skimpy are the outfits?" she asked suspiciously.

"There's one or two tricks where the assistant goes topless."

Her fork dropped to her plate. "Seriously?" she squeaked.

"Yeah."

"But that's...that's objectifying, don't you think?"

"There's nothing objectifying about nudity." His lips pressed together. "It's entertainment."

"I beg your pardon, but if the nudity is just for titillation, which is what you're talking about, then it objectifies the woman who is nude. All she becomes is a pair of tits."

"So I take it you don't approve."

"I-I—" Aside from her gut reaction, she couldn't say with certainty whether she did or not. She'd never given it much thought. Plus, she couldn't say for sure whether it was the topless assistants she really objected to, or if it was the idea of them prancing around in front of Rhys one night after the other. "Whether I approve or not is irrelevant. It's not my act. I guess I just thought your act was good the way it was."

"It was good, but it wasn't taking us where we wanted to go."

"To the top," she verified.

"Yeah."

Melina nodded. It looked like things were lining up for the Dalton family. Although she was happy for them, she couldn't quite picture Rhys living on a cruise ship. Not for very long. But then again, what did she know? After several attempts at eating, she pushed her plate away, no longer having to pretend her stomach hurt.

"Melina, maybe this isn't the best time to ask, but I want to know if—"

"I have to go," she said abruptly.

Rhys's mouth snapped shut. He frowned. "What?"

She raised a shaky hand to her forehead. "I guess I'm feeling worse than I thought. I'd like you to go home now."

"You mean back to the cabin?"

"No. I mean back to Sacramento."

"But the weekend's not over. What about—"

She shook her head. "No worries. You're a genius. I didn't need to learn about technique, I just needed to get my confidence up and be willing to try different things. You made me realize that, and I'll always, always appreciate it. But I think I can take it from here."

He stared at her, his face darkening with something close to anger. "What if I don't want you to go home?"

Her heart began to race. "What do you mean?"

Leaning over, he took her hands in his. "I mean, I've really enjoyed our time together."

"I have to. I suppose Max's plan worked, after all." It

had worked too well.

"Come to Reno with me."

Melina blinked. "What?"

"I know you're supposed to work, but I was hoping you could take some time off."

Whoa. The world seemed to be spinning out of control. He didn't want their time to end either? "Wouldn't I just get in the way?"

"I'd be busy. I have to set up for the show and do rehearsals, but you could hang out. See what it's like. You could visit with Mom and Dad. Then, whenever I could get away…"

She cocked a brow. "What?"

He wiggled his brows up and down, reminding her so much of Max when he was being naughty. "We could get off."

She flushed, not in embarrassment but arousal.

"That certainly sounds tempting." But she'd only be putting off their separation, wouldn't she? And it wouldn't be like it was here. She wouldn't have Rhys's undivided attention. That could be a good thing, but it could also be bad. She adored his parents. They never failed to welcome her in and make her feel a part of the family. Which would make having to leave all the harder. She just couldn't see spending more time with Rhys, knowing pain would once again be waiting for her. So while her heart was screaming, yes, yes, yes, she forced herself to say, "I appreciate the offer, but I'm going to have to say no. I need to get back home and to my lab."

He sat back, and for a moment she thought she saw real distress in his eyes. Then he shrugged. "You're right. What was I thinking? There's way too much to do, getting ready for Seven Seas and all. I should probably put all my focus into that."

"Sure. It's your dream come true, after all."

"Yeah," he whispered.

He put down his napkin, took several bills out of his wallet, and threw them on the table. "You ready to go?"

10

Dalton's Magic Rule #11:
Use your brain and heart as much as your hands.

Back at Rhys's cabin, Melina packed up her things while Rhys put away the mantel and tidied up the house. They'd barely spoken on the drive back from the restaurant, and every time she looked at him she had to force herself not to say, "I changed my mind. Of course I'll go to Reno with you." This was for the best, she told herself for the thousandth time. This weekend was about sexual empowerment, not emotional suicide, and she was lucky Rhys had been part of it.

"You almost ready?"

She whirled around at the sound of Rhys's voice. He stood in the doorway, one hand gripping the header and the other tucked behind his back. She arched a brow. "Is this another pop quiz?"

When he smiled—a genuine smile that showed off his adorable dimple—the relief was disorienting. She hated when things were tense between them, but if he could smile, maybe that meant everything would be okay.

"I suppose in a way it is," he confessed. "I brought your gift with me, but in all the confusion, I don't think I ever wished you a happy birthday."

Playing along, she pretended to think about it. "No. I don't think you did."

"I didn't think so." He stepped into the room. "So are you ready for the question?"

She nodded.

"What's your favorite bug?"

He had to be kidding. "Seriously? What kind of question is that? You already know—"

"Will you just play along?" he gritted out in a long-suffering voice.

"Okay, okay." She took a deep breath. "My favorite bug…" She paused dramatically. "Is the ladybug."

"And why is it your favorite bug?"

"Because of its polka dots," she groaned, remembering the day she'd complained about her mother wanting her to wear a polka dot dress. "But dots on a bug are far different than on a dress. Especially when you're fourteen and fat."

He glared at her. "You weren't fat. You were just…well-cushioned."

She snorted, even though Rhys, unlike Brian, made it sound like a compliment.

"Anyway, maybe you'll feel different about this."

He brought his arm around and held out a small box

wrapped in simple ivory paper. "Happy birthday, Ladybug."

She took the box with trembling fingers and tried to blink back her tears. She didn't quite succeed. One trailed down her cheek, and he swiped it away with his thumb. He didn't question her tears, and she didn't explain them.

Sitting on the bed, she carefully removed the paper and lifted the lid off the box. Her eyes widened in disbelief when she saw what was inside. A small laugh burst out of her. "It's a bikini."

He sat down next to her, his expression watchful, as if he wasn't sure whether she liked it. "Yeah. I saw it when I was in France. The white one you have is a whole lot more daring, but this one…" He shrugged. "I don't know. It just reminded me of you."

She lifted the two pieces out of the box. The material was black, sprinkled with red polka dots. They weren't showy and neither was the cut of the bikini. Unlike the one she'd bought, this one would cover her where she wanted to be covered, yet it was also stylish. Hip. Sexy.

She stroked the fabric as she looked at him. "This is how you see me?"

He frowned a little. "Before I answer, do you like it?"

Happiness swelled within her. Before she could think twice about it, she lunged at him, knocking him back onto the bed even as she squeezed him. "I love it. Thank you."

She kissed him soundly on the mouth, her laughter slowly dying as he cupped her face and brought her lips back to his. He tilted her head to find the right angle, teasing her lips open for his hungry kisses. When he pulled back a little, he smoothed her hair out of her eyes and helped her sit up. "You're as sexy as you're willing to let yourself be. Always remember that, Melina."

He stood and shoved his hands in his pocket. "I'll finish packing and then we can go. Can you give me ten minutes?"

"No," she said abruptly.

He froze and looked over his shoulder at her. "Excuse me?"

Getting quickly to her feet, she set the box with Rhys's gift on the bedroom dresser and placed her hands on her hips. "The bikini's wonderful, but it's not going to make me forget what you promised me yesterday. Or was that just a bunch of talk and no action?"

He was clearly flummoxed by her words as well as her aggressive attitude. "I'm not sure what you're—"

"You said I could tie you up, remember? Granted, I was tired yesterday, but I'm feeling extremely well rested now."

Crossing his arms across his chest, he leaned against the doorjamb. "What about your stomachache?"

"Gone," she said blithely.

"So you want to…" He stared pointedly at the four-poster bed behind her.

"Are you just going to stand there or are you going to get me something to tie you up with?"

"Well, all right, then." He straightened, his lids heavy and intense. "I've got exactly what you need."

* * *

Sitting on Rhys's big bed, Melina tried to give off a carefree, sexy vibe while Rhys retrieved "what she needed" from his magic case. Every thirty seconds, doubt would creep in on her and she'd force herself to look at the bikini, still sitting on the dresser in its gift box. Forget what happened later. She was only going to think about today. Here and now. She and Rhys. And when she wore that bikini to the beach—and she *would* wear it—she would think of him and smile and know that for a short time, she'd had something she never thought she'd have.

Passion. Mutual passion. Even if it didn't come with unicorns and flying dragons, she knew how precious it was now. And she was never going to settle for anything less again.

"I'm baaaaack," Rhys drawled from the doorway, and she sat up. She laughed when she saw rainbows of color fluttering in the air. In each of his hands, he held drapes of silk. Purple and green. Pink and blue.

"They look absolutely decadent," she said.

"Wait until you feel them against your skin."

"Nice try. But I want them against *your* skin. Well, at least some of your skin, anyway."

"And the rest of me?"

A jolt of wickedness shot through her, and she knew it showed on her face when he sucked in a breath. "Let's just say I'll do my very best to make sure not a single inch of you feels neglected."

* * *

Rhys had been sexually active for fifteen years, and in that time he'd often heard talk of pleasure so intense you actually thought you could die from it. He'd never actually experienced it himself. Not until now.

Not until Melina.

Something had changed in her, Rhys thought. He'd seen the insecurity on her face. Had suspected she was about to back off before he'd waved the scarves at her. But whatever doubts she'd had were gone. She seemed determined to touch all of him, taste all of him, drive him mad with desire—and she was doing one hell of a job.

She'd tied his hands and feet to the bed with secure knots that he could still manage to escape, but escape was the last thing he was thinking of. Starting at his feet and working her way up, she'd proved herself to be a woman of her word. Not a single inch of his body had been neglected so far. She'd even discovered an area behind his knee that was an erogenous zone. As she kissed his inner thigh, his cock jerked in anticipation, and he groaned with pleasure when he actually felt sperm well out, undeniable evidence that he was barely hanging on to his control. She smiled when she saw the drop of cum crown his cockhead. "Mmm," she breathed. "Yummy."

"Oh, God," he gasped a second before her mouth slid over him like a hot, slick vice. The lash of her tongue against his slit made his hips arch, and he marveled that he didn't blow the second she started suckling him. The wet noise of her mouth combined with her persistent hums of pleasure. He arched his hips, trying to feed her more of himself, but she focused her attention just on the tip. He strained against the scarves. "Deeper. Take more of me. Please."

She glanced at him from beneath her lashes and instead of taking him deeper, she slowly eased her mouth off him completely. He barely held back his whimper of distress. "Where do you want to be, Rhys? Deeper in my mouth? Or deeper someplace else?"

His eyes widened slightly at her words. At the pure sexual confidence that dripped off them. Tying him down was obviously working for her. And it sure as hell worked for him. "How about we start with your mouth and explore the options from there?"

With a laugh, she bent to place her mouth on him again, but he snapped, "No."

Her confused gaze jerked to his.

Part of him thought he was a fool. How could he deprive himself of even one second of her mouth on him?

But the other part of him was picturing something so magnificent, he couldn't let it go. "Remember what I said before? I'm not just going to lie here and let you pleasure me, Melina."

Now it was her eyes that widened. She pursed her lips as she ran her gaze over his body. "From the looks of things, I don't think you have any choice in the matter."

Damn, he liked her feisty. "You're wrong," he said calmly.

With a challenging arch of one brow, she bent until her breath tickled his cock. Then she took him. Deeply. She worked her mouth over him in every way imaginable. Shallow and deep. Fast and slow. Tenderly and with a wild aggression that allowed him to feel the edge of her teeth against his sensitive shaft and the bite of her nails against his balls. He didn't even try to hold back his moans of pleasure. His throat was actually sore by the time she backed off, her lips red and chapped, her eyes dilated with her own desire.

"Now what was it you were saying about being wrong?"

He had to suck in several breaths before he could speak. "Just biding...my time, baby."

"Is that right?" She gripped him tightly and stroked him. He knew he was about thirty seconds from shooting his load all over her hand.

"That's right," he said, struggling to sound in control. "Because I can see your pussy juice glistening on your thighs. And I'm going to lick it up even as you take my cock in your mouth again. You ever do the sixty-nine, Melina?"

He wasn't surprised when she licked her lips and shook her head. "It never looked particularly appealing to me."

"That's something else you need a lesson on. Now put yourself over me. I've worked up quite an appetite in the past few minutes."

She hesitated and released him. "Rhys, why don't I—"

"Now, Melina," he said firmly. He knew why most women didn't like doing the sixty-nine. It exposed them. Made them feel unsure of themselves. Awkward. He wanted everything Melina was. The confidence and the insecurity. The grace and the awkwardness. But there'd be no hiding for her, just like there'd be no hiding for him. "I want you against me. Over me. On my tongue. And it's what you want, too, isn't it?"

"Yes," she whispered.

"Then give us what we both want, baby."

Moving slowly, she got in position. He waited until she seemed comfortable. Until she tentatively took him inside her mouth again. Until she started to lose herself in the act of pleasing him.

Then, raising his head, he buried his face in her sweet muskiness. Lapping gently, he swiped through the drenched folds left vulnerable by her recent waxing. Deliberately, he stayed away from the hard knot that crested her core until she was pushing herself down on him and begging. He gave her what she wanted, manipulating her clit with his tongue and teeth until she was sobbing. At the same time, her mouth tightened on his cock as she tried to draw the cum out of his balls.

His body tightened when the pleasure came rushing at him. Before he exploded, he managed to plunge his tongue inside her, detonating her own release so it coincided perfectly with his. In that instance, his entire world became Melina. He shouted her name even as she shouted his.

11

Dalton's Magic Rule #12:
When all else fails, pull out the rabbit.

"Tell me you're joking, Max. Please."

At Rhys's urgent tone, Melina's eyes popped open. Her gaze quickly swept the room, taking in the scarves that still dangled from the bedposts, as well as her packed suitcase next to the bedroom door, which was cracked open slightly. Sitting up gingerly, she swung her legs off the bed and quickly put on her clothes.

She opened the door and saw Rhys pacing as he talked on his cell phone.

"Can't they wait until after the Seven Seas performance?" He paused, ran a hand through his hair, then began pacing again. "I know you can't time something like that, but she signed a contract. No, I'm not saying I'm going to sue her, but what does she expect us to do? We hired her specifically because she was shorter than the other girls. That's what the act needs—someone who's about five-four." He scoffed, held the phone away from him as if he wanted to throw it against the wall, then snapped it back up to his ear. "Do you know how much time it would take to modify it? Well, I do. A lot."

At his increasing distress, Melina stepped out of the room and caught his eye. She motioned to him in a "what's going on?" gesture. He briefly closed his eyes, held up a finger, then told Max, "I'm in Lake Shasta with Melina. I've got to get her home and then I'll catch my flight. I'll see you there before midnight." He paused, glancing at Melina before he quietly said, "No."

He disconnected the call.

"I'm sorry about that. I've got to leave immediately and do some damage control."

"One of your assistants can't perform?"

"She's decided to show her ex that she's serious about reconciliation and that means she's quitting traveling immediately."

"And she's the only girl who can assist with the trick?"

He pinched the bridge of his nose, his eyes all scrunched up as if he was in pain. "Yeah."

"Can't you just do a different trick?"

"Sure. It's just this trick is pretty spectacular. I think if we nailed it, we'd blow Seven Seas out of the water. Without it..." He sighed and shook his head. "I don't know if it'll be enough. We're competing against some pretty good acts, including the Salvador brothers. They'll be unveiling a new trick, too."

Appearing as if he'd suddenly lost the strength to stand, he moved to the sofa, dropped onto it, leaned his head back, and stared at the ceiling. He looked so defeated that she rushed to sit beside him and hold his hand.

"I worked so hard on this one. But, hey," he said, looking at her with a strained smile. "Maybe this is a sign that the sea's not for me. We've got our established circuit. We'll just keep working at it."

"Why is this contract so important to you? Sure, it's prestigious, but you're so successful already."

"It's not just the prestige. It's having the best of both worlds, or as close as you can get. Stability as well as the thrill of performing. Even if that stability's on a cruise ship, it's still better than packing up and then unpacking again every few weeks."

She looked around her, at the house Rhys had restored and essentially kept to himself. His complexity was also his weakness. How could he fulfill his thirst for adventure when he equally craved roots to hold him down? She supposed Seven Seas was the perfect solution.

"I'm so sorry, Rhys," she said, not knowing what else to say. "But I'm sure your other tricks will wow Seven Seas, too."

He took a deep breath and patted her hand absently. "Thanks." His eyes focused, as if he was actually seeing her for the first time since she'd walked out of the bedroom. He kissed her gently. "Thank you for everything." Closing his eyes, he leaned his forehead against her, his breaths steady and quiet. Finally, he lifted his head. "You ready?" He got to his feet and held out his hand.

She automatically took it and stood, even as she strained to think of a solution to Rhys's problem. There must be something they could do. That *she* could do.

She froze. What she was thinking seemed almost laughable, but what other options did they have? She gripped his hand. "Rhys, you said Seven Seas is coming for one of your shows. Which one?"

"The opening night. This Wednesday."

"So that's the one that's really important in terms of that particular trick."

"Yeah, but like I said, the chances of modifying the apparatus by then are slim."

"What if you don't have to modify it? Can you just train someone who's the right size?"

"I suppose, but who am I going to find now?" He shook his head. "Like I said, we'll figure it—"

"I'm five-four."

He released her hand. "Huh?"

"I said, I'm five-four. I can...I can stand in for your assistant if that would help. I'm sure I'm heavier than her, though. And I'm absolutely not a performer, but..."

She trailed off. He didn't say anything. He didn't move. He just stared at her, his expression stunned. She could feel herself turning red with embarrassment. "You know, it was a stupid idea—"

"You'd do that for me?" he asked. "Get up in front of a theater of strangers and let me tie you up?"

"Well, I'd rather not think of the strangers right now—
"

"What about work? You said you had to get back, and to have a shot of pulling it off, I'd need you right away so we could rehearse."

"When would you need me by?"

"Tonight. Tomorrow at the latest."

"So you can drive me home, I'll pack, call into work in the morning, and fly out tomorrow."

"Why would you do that?"

She moved toward him, not stopping until she was close enough to take his hands and kiss them. "How can you ask me that? I know how much this contract means to you. If I can do anything to help you get it, I will." She dropped her hands and stepped back. "I feel a little silly, though. I mean, me on stage? If you want to say thank you and forget it, I understand."

He took her hands again. "Thank you," he said. "And I think—"

He paused, and she held her breath, waiting for him to reject her.

"I think you'll be perfect on stage."

All she felt was relief. And joy. "Really?"

"Yes."

She jumped up and down in her excitement, her insecurity momentarily forgotten. "Okay, then let's do it."

She broke away from him and rushed to her bedroom to get her suitcase. He turned to get his own stuff, stopping when she called out, "Oh, and Rhys?"

"Yeah?"

"I just want to make something perfectly clear."

Wariness crossed his face. "What?"

"I'm absolutely not doing anything topless."

His mouth quirked. "You sure? Because, man, with your body, we would definitely draw in some—"

"Rhys…" she drawled warningly.

"Okay, sure. No going topless. But that only applies on stage, right?"

"You have somewhere else in mind?"

"Oh, I've definitely got several places in mind."

Her eyes rounded. "As long as we don't have an audience, I think we can make things work."

"That's fine with me. I do my best work one-on-one, anyway."

12

Dalton's Magic Rule #13:
Draw out the tension until the big finish.

"Let me get this straight," Lucy insisted. "He actually got you to do a sixty-nine, and you liked it?"

Melina tossed another shirt into her suitcase before she turned back to her friend. "Yes, Lucy, he did. Y-E-S. And, yes, I did. The answers are the same no matter how many times you ask the questions. Now, can we please talk about more pressing matters? Like how I'm going to get on stage without puking and single-handedly ruining Rhys's shot at this contract?"

From her spot on the bed, Grace fanned herself with both hands. "I don't know, darlin'. After what you described, how can you think of anything other than when you can jump him next?"

"On the other hand," Lucy interjected, "think about how grateful he's going to be after you help him land that cruise gig. My God, the man will probably do anything you ask him to. A-ny-thing."

Melina shook her head. "Will you two stop? You should have seen his face when I said I'd help him. He wants that contract—he needs it—and he's relying on me. What if I can't do it? What if I let him down?"

"What if unicorns and flying dragons really do exist?" Lucy shot back. "Why are you focusing on the show and the contract Rhys may or may not get? You had mind-blowing, head-banging sex with your fantasy guy, and he's obviously in love with you."

Melina sat down on the bed next to Grace, only to fall backward and stare at the ceiling. "Believe me, the sex isn't far from my mind. But where do you get he's in love with me?"

"He asked you to go to Reno with him before Max called," Grace pointed out.

Biting her lip, she sat up. "You really think he's in love with me?"

"Yes," Lucy said.

"Definitely," agreed Grace.

"Then why wouldn't he just say so?" Melina asked softly.

"Why haven't you told him that you love him?" Lucy countered.

Wide-eyed, Melina stared at her. "Because I'm afraid."

"Of what? He's not going to reject you. The guy bought you a rocking bikini in France, for God's sake!"

"I'm afraid he'll walk away anyway," she insisted.

Lucy opened her mouth to respond, but it was Grace who countered, "No, you're not, Melina. You're afraid he'll walk away and ask you to come with him. And you're not sure you love him enough to do it."

Melina and Lucy stared at her. Lucy turned to Melina. "Is that true?"

"No. I mean..." Melina closed her eyes and forced herself to look deep within herself for the answer. She opened her eyes and glared at Grace. "God, I hate it when you do that."

Lucy dropped onto the bed beside her. "I'm confused."

"Well, so am I," Melina snapped. Standing, she paced the small area between her bed and her dresser. "Grace is right. When we're together, I can't imagine being without him. But when we're apart, I can't imagine fitting into his world. I'm not even sure I want to. Sure, it sounds exciting, but I'm a homebody at heart. I'd like to travel more, but only if I have a home to come back to. Someplace to raise my children and make memories. I know now that Rhys wants some version of that, too, but I just can't see myself on the road or on the sea, hanging out in the shadows and waiting for him to finish one performance after another."

"So all this time, it hasn't been about whether you could satisfy him or whether he could love you," Lucy said. "You're saying that even if those things are golden, you're still not sure it'll work out?"

"Those things were definitely real fears, but even

without them, yes. I guess I am saying that."

For the first time Melina could remember, Lucy didn't seem to know what to say.

That was so not okay.

"So what do I do?" Melina cried.

Grace knelt in front of her and took her hands in hers. "You're already doing it, sweetie. You're leaving your world and venturing into his. No speculating about what it's like anymore. No wondering whether you'll like it. One way or another, you're going to find out the answer to that pop quiz. Being with him would require you to change your whole life. If you decide you don't want to do that, then he's not the guy for you. So what? Maybe Jamie is."

"Please." Lucy rolled her eyes. "She just got through saying she wasn't settling for passionless sex again. Professor Jamie Whitcomb isn't the type to inspire passion in any woman. He's too damn arrogant and uptight for his own good."

Melina studied her friend, forgetting her own troubles for a second. "Where's all this hostility coming from? I thought you barely knew Jamie."

"Oh, I know him all right."

When she didn't elaborate, Melina turned to Grace.

"Turns out the dean wants Lucy's department represented at the conference tomorrow, as well," Grace explained. "Since Jamie's coordinating it..."

Melina gasped. Holy shit. The conference. She gripped Grace's hands. "The conference. I'm supposed to speak with Jamie. He's depending on me."

Lucy waved her hand dismissively. "Oh, please. Like anyone'll miss you." She didn't miss Melina's glare. "You know what I mean. You've got a PowerPoint presentation set up, right? Either Jamie can pick up the slack or someone else can."

"You," Melina said at the same time she thought it.

Looking at her like she was crazy, Lucy laughed and held out her hand. "Excuse me? I don't think so. I have to attend the conference—against my will, I might add—in order to network at the reception. But I wasn't planning on attending any of the presentations beforehand."

"You can do my presentation with your hands tied behind your back. You're a quick study, and you have no problem speaking in public."

"I'm not an entomologist," Lucy exclaimed, beginning to look a little panicked. "I don't know a thing about bugs."

Melina rushed to her desk in the living room and returned to the bedroom with a folder, neatly organized and tabbed. "You don't have to. Like you said, everything's set up. You just have to read my notes. Please, Lucy?"

"I-I…" Looking like a hunted rabbit, Lucy turned to Grace.

"I'm out of town that day," Grace said quickly.

"Please, Lucy. He's not my soul mate, but I like Jamie and respect him. I can't just ditch him. This conference is a huge deal and, as the organizer, he's going to be swamped. Do this for me, and I'll owe you, I promise."

"You'll owe me, huh?" Lucy said, still looking like she'd rather eat dirt.

Melina just nodded and held out the folder.

With a sigh, Lucy took it. "Fine. I'll keep you in Jamie's good graces just in case you decide you don't want Rhys as much as you thought."

"It's not Rhys I'm unsure about," Melina insisted. "Not anymore."

"Honey, it's all part of the package, right? You can't have Rhys without all the rest."

After her friends left, Melina thought about what Lucy had said. She thought about it as she finished packing. She thought about it when she boarded the plane the next morning. And she thought about it as she walked outside to meet Rhys.

When she saw Rhys, she dropped her luggage and ran into his arms, almost crying with relief when his arms wrapped around her and pulled her in close. She lifted her face to kiss him just as his mouth covered hers. His tongue sank into her mouth, stealing her breath and her sanity until she finally pulled away.

She opened her mouth and tried to say it: *I love you. I want to spend the rest of my life with you. If that means going on the road or living out of a suitcase for the rest of my life, I'll do it.* Instead, she just kissed him again.

"You ready to get to work?" he asked with a grin.

She forced a smile. "You tie me up. You work your magic. I just need to smile and look pretty, right? How hard can it be?"

* * *

Jillian knocked on the dressing room door even louder this time. "Aren't you ready yet?"

Melina stared at herself in the full-length mirror, cringing at what she saw. The sparkly outfit that Jillian was trying to alter to fit her form was her exact size, only Rhys's runaway assistant had obviously had more to love on top than she did. Instead of enhancing her minimal curves, the droopy neckline made her look flatter than an ironing board, and the minuscule skirt made her thighs look like tree trunks.

"I told you, it doesn't fit," Melina called out again, wondering if the woman was hard of hearing.

"Of course it doesn't," Jillian called, her voice clearly reflecting her impatience. "I'm not done with it yet. Now come out here so you can get back to practice."

Melina groaned. Practice. Right.

She and Rhys had been practicing ever since they'd arrived from the airport. Not that he was a slave driver. He'd given her plenty of breaks, for food and for nookie, but as soon as they started practicing again, it was all business. Her body ached from having to stretch out and hang for so long from the Metamorphosis apparatus, and she was jittery because of the way Rhys repeatedly ran his hands up and down her body.

"Usually I don't think anything of doing this," he'd

said. "It's all just in a day's work." Before she could snort and call him a liar, he kissed her neck and whispered in her ear, "Doing it to you reminds me of something."

She'd swallowed and breathed out, "What's that?"

"I owe you for torturing me when I was tied up. When you're spread out in front me and unable to do anything but beg for me to take you, remember that."

Closing her eyes, she licked her lips. "I'm doing you a favor here. I don't think threats are appropriate at this point. Besides, I thought you liked what we did."

He'd just chuckled and backed off, releasing her to wardrobe.

Knowing she couldn't put it off any longer, she opened the door and peeked out. Jillian whirled around and waved her closer. "Come on out so I can see what I'm working with."

Reluctantly, Melina stepped into view.

Instead of laughing her ass off, as Melina had expected, Jillian nodded. "Good. That's good."

"Good?" Melina echoed in astonishment. "I look like a pear shoved into a seventies-era tube top."

"You leave it to me. By the time I'm done with this costume, you'll look like you were born to walk that stage."

"Yeah, except I won't be doing much walking. More like hanging," she mumbled, then felt like a whiny fool. She was hanging with Rhys and for Rhys, that's all that should matter.

It was if Jillian could read her mind. "Yes, well, that's

what women do for the men they love."

Melina automatically shook her head. "I'm just doing a friend a favor."

Now Jillian did laugh. "Okay, honey. But don't worry about it. It doesn't matter that they've never dated anyone more than six weeks. We all fall in love with one of those boys at some time or another. Not all of us are lucky enough to get that love returned, that's all."

"From what I hear, they've done plenty of loving to go around."

Jillian shot her a disappointed look. "You are supposed to be the smart one, right?"

Before Melina could do more than gasp, Rhys's mother, Rachel, swept in. They'd already visited several times, but it was still a nice surprise to see her again. The way she hugged Melina suggested she felt the same. "So what do you think, Jillian? Didn't we tell you Melina is an absolute doll?"

Nodding, Jillian tugged at Melina's dress and adjusted pins here and there. "She sure is. A little dubious about your boys' reputation with the ladies, but other than that, she's fine by me."

Melina blushed and tried to stammer out a reply, but Jillian just planted her hands on her hips and eyed her up and down. "Yep. The crowd's going to love her," she declared.

"Let's just hope Seven Seas does." Rhys's mother looked at her watch. "You've got enough time for one more rehearsal, Melina, but Rhys says you've caught on really fast. He's quite impressed with you, young lady."

"What's Rhys doing now?" she asked, trying to appear only casually interested.

"He's rehearsing on the main stage with Max and the other girls."

"Can I go in and watch?"

"Of course!" Rachel exclaimed. "You're one of the crew now."

One of the crew. As Melina peeled out of her horrid costume and dressed, a smile crept across her face. Despite some lingering nerves, part of her was starting to *feel* like part of the crew. Everyone was friendly and had welcomed her with open arms, chattering with her about their families and the excitement they felt about getting the Seven Seas contract.

As she rushed to the main stage, Melina thought about what Jillian had said. That everyone fell in love with Rhys or Max at some point, but only a special few were lucky enough to have that love returned. She'd known Rhys and Max loved her since she was fourteen years old. Despite the ups and downs between them, she'd known she could count on them if she ever needed them. Her presence proved they could do the same.

Taking care to be quiet as she opened the heavy doors to the theater, she sneaked into the very back row and watched as Rhys performed one trick after another. There were two other female assistants who assisted in the act. Having hung from the Metamorphosis apparatus and seen Rhys's complicated new trick for herself, she now knew why he required a female assistant of shorter stature. That wasn't true for his other tricks.

The two other girls, introduced to her as Amanda and Tina, were close to six feet, their bodies thin yet curvy, especially in the chest area. Amanda had long, multi-hued blonde hair, and Tina had a wavy red bob that looked perpetually disheveled. They were model gorgeous, and it would have been easy to hate them both but for the fact they were extremely nice and down-to-earth. Amanda had a degree in nursing, and Tina wore crystals and had offered to give Melina a tarot reading. She liked them, even if they did make her feel like the dumpy nerd who didn't quite belong.

With a flourish, Rhys finished one trick, then switched places with Max, who'd been sitting in a chair at the side of the stage. She hadn't spent a lot of time with Max, other than to scold him, then kiss him, for what he'd done at the hotel. She hadn't brought up Trisha or the incident from twelve years ago, and neither had Rhys. Still, she could tell Max was feeling awkward about things. He was more quiet than usual and, except for rehearsals, he kept mostly to himself. She'd asked Rhys about it, but he'd just shrugged, saying Max could be moody but that he'd eventually snap out of it.

The music cued and another trick began, everyone flowing around the stage like they were born to be there. At one point, Rhys called out for them to stop, and he and Max discussed something while the girls left the stage. Melina felt so proud as she watched them. They were good at what they did, and it was obvious that while Max and Rhys were a team, Rhys made things happen. He kept things running. He was the heart of the Dalton Twins' Magic Act. Without him, it couldn't possibly survive. More important, he clearly loved what he did. Being around his family and performing with them gave him a spark and vitality that had been missing before, even when he'd been relaxed and having fun in Lake Shasta.

Knowing she didn't have much time before she'd be called to the stage herself, Melina got to her feet and quietly made her way toward the exit. She was almost there when she saw Amanda and Tina return.

They were topless, their big breasts round and thrust out for everyone to see. Rhys and Max glanced up, then kept talking, obviously unfazed by their nudity.

Melina, on the other hand, felt the ground drop out from under her. Bracing herself with a shaky hand, she slowly lowered herself into another seat. She watched as Max performed one illusion after another, the whole time keeping at least one of the girls close. He touched them often, almost absently, a hand on a hip here, or a caress against the side of a breast there. Melina knew it was all for show—that it didn't mean anything to any of them— but she couldn't help thinking of the way Rhys had touched her when they'd practiced, too. And even though it wasn't *him* touching the girls now, she knew he and Max traded off performing every trick, so he'd touched them at some point and would continue to do so.

Someone touched her shoulder, and she jerked her

head around. Rhys stood beside her, his mouth grim. "Hey," he said.

She turned back to the stage. "Hi," she whispered.

He lowered himself to the seat beside her and sighed. "I warned you there were a couple of acts that contained nudity, Melina."

Nodding, she licked her lips. "Yeah. You did. You didn't tell me how often you got to cop a feel, though." As soon as the bitter words left her mouth, she wanted to call them back. But she couldn't. And she couldn't pretend it wasn't how she felt. Not so much because the touching was sexual or even offensive, but because it seemed to highlight just how different their lives really were.

He lightly grasped her arms and turned her to face him. "It's just an act. The equivalent of an on-screen kiss. It doesn't mean anything."

"I know that." But it means something to me, she thought. *And this is what he'd be doing, night after night, while I wait for him. While I give up my life for him.* She was an insecure person during the best of times. How low would she stoop if she had to imagine Rhys's hands on another woman's body every night?

She stood. "I was just going to get something to eat before we rehearse. What time should I be back?"

"Melina, can we talk about this?"

"There's nothing to talk about," she said with a thin smile. "This is your life, and there's nothing wrong with it. Now what time do you want me back?"

"We'll rehearse in an hour. Does that work?"

"An hour's good."

She tried to move past him, but there wasn't enough room unless she wanted to squeeze by and brush against him. Knowing it was silly, she turned and walked down the other side of the aisle, slipping outside through another door.

She didn't look back, but she never got something to eat, either. Instead, feeling more like an outsider than ever, she wandered the streets outside the theater until she came to a nest of shops. One in particular caught her eye, and she stopped to stare at the display window.

The mannequin decked out in leather should have looked ridiculous, but to Melina it represented the daring, almost surreal nature of Rhys's celebrity lifestyle. Foreign. Exotic. Out of reach.

Yet, she reminded herself that she'd been enjoying her time here. That she'd begun to acclimate to his world. So what if she'd suffered a slight bump in the road? Why couldn't she don the leather outfit in the window just as she had Jillian's stage costume? Although it probably wouldn't feel right at first, she'd eventually grow accustomed to it. Wouldn't she?

At the very least, Rhys would know she was willing to try. Maybe, regardless of her reaction to his topless assistants, things could work out for them.

Maybe she just needed to prove it to herself, and this hollow feeling of despair would vanish forever.

But if she was going to take risks, she wasn't going to be the only one. Rhys had allowed himself to be vulnerable when he'd let her tie him up, but things had gotten significantly more complicated since then. If she was going to strip herself bare for him, then he was going to do the same. Only then would she believe the depth of his feelings for her.

With newfound resolve, Melina walked into the store.

* * *

That night, after rehearsal was finally over, Rhys practically speed-walked back to his hotel. He was exhausted. Hungry. Grumpy. None of that compared to the desperate need he had to see Melina and confirm that things were okay between them.

When he'd noticed her at the back of the theater, her eyes on Max and the topless assistants, he'd felt like he'd been punched in the stomach. She'd looked so sad. Defeated. Nothing like the woman who'd been gamely trying to adjust to the foreign world she'd been shoved into.

He'd been a mess after that. Distracted. Edgy. But when she'd shown up for practice, Melina had seemed to be back to her regular self. She'd laughed when he'd teased her, and she'd given him a nice, long kiss before she'd left the theater, saying she'd have a surprise for him back at the room.

Now, two hours later, all he wanted was to crawl into Melina's arms. He wasn't even nervous about tomorrow's show. Whatever the outcome, he just wanted to know what his future with Melina had in store.

He was going to do what he should have done a long time ago. He was going to give Melina a choice—home and hearth, or him. And it didn't matter whether it was fair or not, but he was going to do everything in his power to make sure she chose him.

When he opened the door to their suite, he did so quietly, in case Melina was sleeping. Sure enough, the bedroom was dark, quiet except for the steady buzz of the air conditioner. He shut the door, then flicked on the bathroom light so he could undress. When he saw Melina, he froze.

"Melina?"

Music with a slow, hip-thrusting beat began to play. From her seat in the corner, Melina stood and walked toward him, her hips swaying exaggeratedly, her steps keeping time with the music. He nearly swallowed his tongue when he saw the crisscrossed laces running between her plumped-up breasts. Was she wearing a corset?

She was. It wasn't just any corset, either. It was made of soft black leather that molded itself to her curves. She wore a matching dog collar and wrist bands; no spikes, thank God, just silver eyelets that matched the ones on her chest. Makeup, more makeup than he'd ever seen her wear, layered her face, making her look like a stranger. A beautiful, tempting, lustful stranger, but a stranger nonetheless.

She looked at him challengingly, crooked her finger,

and urged him closer.

He didn't move. "Where'd you get that?" he asked hoarsely.

"There are plenty of shops around." Spreading her legs wide, she planted her fists on her hips, a cocky, Superwoman stance that called attention to the four-inch spike heels she was wearing. "What do you think?"

What did he think? Not much, since all his blood had rushed straight to his dick. "You look..." He paused, knowing "like a stranger" wasn't the right thing to say. "Hot. You look hot. But you'll be even more hot when you're naked."

She pouted and shook her head. "Nice of you to say, but I'm not the one who's going to be stripping down. You are."

"Oh, am I?" He couldn't help but think of the night he'd walked into his Sacramento hotel room and found her waiting for him. Other than the unexpectedness of it, that had felt right. Something here was off, but he couldn't quite put his finger on what it was.

"Yep." Pulling out a chair, she slowly turned it until she could straddle it, her legs spread wide, the bottomless crotch of her outfit revealing that tiny strip of hair that drove him mad. He hissed in a breath and started jerking at buttons.

Whatever the hell was going on here, they'd deal with it. Afterward. Ripping off his shirt, he stalked closer.

"Stop," she commanded.

He did, even as he clenched his fists and sucked in air

like a locomotive.

"Perform for me. Strip for me." Her voice sounded harsh. Demanding. A little bitchy. Even as his erection lengthened, a part of him resisted.

"It's been a long night, baby. I don't think I'm up—"

"Oh, you're up, all right. And you're going to stay up. For as long as I want you to be. Now strip."

Hands shaking, he unbuttoned his pants and swept them off, along with his socks and shoes. When he was done, he crossed his arms over his chest, eyes half-hooded. "Now what?"

She stood and pointed to the chair she'd vacated. "Now you sit here. Put your hands behind your back."

"Melina—"

"Do it."

He sighed and sat down. Immediately, she straddled him, rubbing her sweet flesh against his dick, making him wet with her juices even as she raised up on her tiptoes, shoved her chest under his chin, and leaned forward to bind his wrists together. He bent his head to nuzzle her and breathe in her scent when it dawned on him that she wasn't using scarves but handcuffs. "What—"

He rattled the handcuffs, but she shook her head. She tauntingly held a key out to him. "Uh-uh. No tricks tonight, Rhys. It's just you and me. Remember how you said I tortured you? Well, I'm finding that one taste isn't enough for me. I want to torture you some more."

He'd never been so pissed off and so turned on at the same time. Clenching his teeth, he reminded her, "You're due for some torturing yourself. More and more with each second that passes. Now, get these off me."

"What's wrong? The magician can't get them off himself? Looks like you'll just have to take what I dish out."

She sank to her knees in front of him, pushing apart his thighs, and positioned herself between them.

He tightened them around her warningly, not enough to hurt her but enough to let her know he wasn't playing. "Release me. Now, Melina. I'm not kidding."

She moved her hands to the curve of his ass and dared to dip her finger into the crevice. Then she leaned down, looking up at him the whole time, and took him in her mouth. She ate him like she was starved for it. She licked him like he was an ice cream cone and she was burning up. She cupped his balls and raked her fingertips up the length of him even as she worked the tip of him with her tongue, alternately flicking him and then sucking him. She gave him head like she'd been doing it for years, seven days a week, twenty-four hours a day, practicing it time and again in preparation for this very moment so she could drive him utterly insane.

When his shouts of pleasure faded, she wiped her mouth, caught a drop of cum that had managed to elude her, then licked it off. He groaned, barely able to move, and not just because of the cuffs. "Kiss me," he whispered, needing to be close to her. Needing something that he couldn't even name.

To his astonishment, she shook her head. Smoothing

out her corset, she sauntered in her four-inch fuck-me heels to the bathroom. When she returned, she was carrying a crop. His eyes widened in disbelief.

"I picked up a few other things while I was out." She brought the crop down on her ass and pouted. "Maybe if you're a good boy, you can spank me later."

It was all too much for him. The makeup. Her cool taunting. The way she refused to kiss him or give him an ounce of her softness. With a powerful surge, he stood. As he did, his bound hands slipped over the chair back and, in a move that left Melina gaping at him, he slipped his bound hands in front of him.

She blinked her eyes several times, as if she wasn't quite sure what had happened. "How'd you—"

"I guess you didn't know I was double-jointed. It's come in handy a time or two." He held his arms out and pinned her with a furious glare. "Unlock them."

She shook her head, backing away from him. When she bumped into the door, he grabbed her wrists in his hands and raised them above her head. Then, with a tug, he pulled her around and threw her onto the bed. He had her covered with his body and pinned down in less than three seconds.

"What the hell was that about?" he gritted out, trying to regain control even though his wrists were still manacled.

She struggled beneath him, her attempts to get away very real. "Unpredictability," she spat. "I thought you'd like it."

"The outfit I like. But not the makeup. Not the attitude. I don't want to fuck a sexy stranger. I want to fuck you. I fucking love you, Melina. Don't you get that by now?"

The fight left her immediately, and tears filled her eyes. "What do you want from me? I'm trying to fit in. I'm trying to give you the excitement the other women in your life have given you."

He clenched his teeth. "No one has given me what you have, Melina. No one. You make me feel things that no one else can. Right now, that includes making me fucking furious, but I love you all the same. That's not going to change, and you don't have to change who you are because you're afraid it will."

"But that's because we're here and because it's all new. What happens when you realize I don't fit in? What happens when you lose interest? 'Cause you will lose interest, Rhys. You always do."

"What the hell does that mean?"

"You've never dated someone more than six weeks."

"Who told you that crap?"

She pressed her lips together.

Abruptly, Rhys released her and stood. Warily, silently, she retrieved the keys and released the handcuffs. He dressed. When he fastened his belt, he turned to her.

"I noticed you didn't respond to my declaration of love. How am I supposed to interpret that?"

She sat up. Reached for her robe and put it on. "I've told you before that I love you."

"Yeah, but at the same time you said you love Max. So what's it going to be Melina? I love you. I know my life isn't what you would choose, but I have other people to consider. I want to know: Do you love me and do you want to be a part of my life, whatever that entails?"

"Whatever that entails." She sniffed derisively. "You don't ask for much, do you?"

His shoulders dropped, and he stared at the floor. "And that's not a very encouraging answer, is it?"

"You can't just—"

They both jumped when someone pounded on the door. "Rhys! Melina. Open up. We've got trouble."

It was Max. Melina jumped to her feet as Rhys answered the door.

Max strode in. After taking in Melina's makeup and eyebrow-raising outfit, as well as their grim expressions, he shook his head. "Great. I can see things are going swell in here, too."

"What is it?"

Max eyes radiated regret. "Someone got into the theater after practice. I came back because I'd forgotten to lock up and..."

"And what?" Rhys prompted.

"And the Metamorphosis rack's been destroyed."

Melina gasped and immediately covered her mouth with both hands.

"What?" Rhys whispered. He dropped into the chair that still sat prominently displayed in the center of the room. He saw Melina move toward him, then stop. That hurt more than what Max had to say next.

"Someone took an ax to it. It's in pieces. There's no way you'll be able to fix it. Not before the show tomorrow."

* * *

Two days later, Melina was in her lab, trying to focus on her current experiment. It was a little tough when her eyes kept tearing up and she had to excuse herself yet again so she could cry in private.

She'd called Max first thing this morning, and he'd told her that Seven Seas had decided to book the Salvador brothers as their permanent act. When Melina had asked about Rhys, Max had laughed bitterly. "Rhys's gonna be fine, Melina. He'll bounce back with something that will make Seven Seas come crawling back to us on their knees, I guarantee it. Recovering from what you did to him isn't going to be quite so easy."

She'd stiffened at the censure in his tone. "Me? I didn't—"

"You couldn't get away from here fast enough, could you? The moment you weren't needed for the act, you left."

"I talked to you and Rhys. I asked you if you needed me for anything, and you both said no. Rhys wouldn't even talk to me."

"He was upset, and when he's upset he withdraws. That's just how he is. He told me what happened in your room before I interrupted."

She sucked in her breath, appalled. Rhys had told Max about her corset and crop? The handcuffs? She nearly moaned in horror, but Max kept talking.

"He told me he asked you to stay with him. That he loved you. And that you threw it back in his face."

"I-I didn't," she protested. "I did no such thing. I just...I just didn't have a chance to answer. You came into the room and everything was a mess and—"

"And you got on a plane and flew home. That was your answer, Melina. And Rhys knows it."

By the time she'd hung up with Max, Melina had almost been paralyzed with doubt. She'd only wanted to get home so she could think, but had getting on the plane been her answer? Wasn't she entitled to think things through before she changed her life so drastically? She was still questioning herself, what she'd done, and what she wanted when she returned to the lab. Instead of work flying by like it normally did, the hours passed painfully slow, and even then she'd gotten next to nothing done.

When she got home, she had a message on her machine. Her heart beating fast, she played it back, hoping it was Rhys. It was her mother, telling her to call her right away.

Melina picked up the phone and dialed the number her mother had left.

Her mother answered the phone.

"Hi, Mom," she said.

"Hi, honey. Thanks for calling me back. We'll only

have access to a phone for a couple of days until the Vietnam tour starts."

"Vietnam? I thought you were still in China?"

"We left China days ago, dear. Now, tell me, how are you?"

Melina swallowed hard and tried to answer calmly. Instead, she released a ragged, pain-filled sob.

"Oh, no. Honey, what's wrong?"

It all poured out of her. Her feelings for Rhys. The challenge Grace had thrown down. Max's set up with the rooms. The lake and the incredible sex and the way Melina had alternately felt welcomed and alienated once they'd arrived in Reno. By the time she'd stopped talking, her voice was raspy. There was only silence on the other end of the line.

Melina covered her eyes with her hand, appalled that she'd just unloaded on her quiet, reserved mother, especially when she was so far away and couldn't do anything to help anyway. "It's okay," she reassured her. "*I'm* okay. I just need to accept who I am and what I want. You did that. That's why you left acting, isn't it? Because you were more suited to the type of life Daddy led."

"Oh, please, Melina," her mother said. "You don't really believe that, do you?"

"What do you mean?"

"I did not leave acting because that life didn't suit me. I left it because I thought that's what I needed to do in order to keep your father. His parents were very conservative and didn't approve of acting. To them, it was

213

the same thing as being a whore. I wanted their approval almost as much as I wanted your father. So I gave up my passion for acting and was fortunate to be blessed with a different kind of passion."

"Passion again," she murmured. Her mother was describing exactly what Melina had told Lucy didn't exist. Inside her, hope fluttered its wings like a butterfly just emerging from its cocoon. "So that's what I should do? I mean, you're obviously happy. You don't have regrets—"

Her mother laughed. "Honey, I have plenty of regrets. And I'm certainly not telling you to follow in my footsteps and give up your life just to be with Rhys."

"So you're saying I was right to come back?"

"No."

"No," Melina echoed. Frustration made her next words harsher than she intended. "Well, what are you saying, Mom? Because I need to know what's the right thing to do."

"There is no right or wrong answer, Melina. Things will be what you demand they be."

Pulling the phone from her ear, she stared at it, certain a foreign creature must have inhabited her mother's body. Her mother didn't talk like that. Rhys did.

Walking into the living room, she put the phone back to her ear. "I don't understand," she breathed. She picked up the picture of Max and Rhys with their dates, the one she'd focused on before propositioning Max. "I'm looking at a picture of Rhys and Max after they won their award in Vegas. They're with their dates, and I...I'm having a hard time picturing myself with them."

"That's because you're looking at the wrong picture. You've got tons of pictures with just you and Rhys. Pull those out and look at them. Ask yourself what you see."

"I know what I'll see. Me. As plain and boring as ever." But she wasn't a dominatrix either, at least not one who liked to wear leather and use a crop. Not when Rhys wasn't into it. Even now, she winced at how she'd treated him, acting cold because she'd wanted him to feel as vulnerable as she did.

"If that's what you see, you're focusing on the wrong person. Instead of focusing on yourself, focus on Rhys. Then ask yourself what you see."

"But Mom—"

"I'm sorry, sweetie, but I have to go. I love you."

Her mother hung up, leaving Melina to ponder her final words. She put down the framed picture of Rhys and Max, and pulled out the boxes of loose photos she kept under her bed. Then she laid a bunch out, pulling out the ones that showed her with Rhys. Since she'd known him for years, there were enough to cover her queen bedspread. She walked around the bed, studying them, trying to ignore her own image and whether she looked fat or was having a bad-hair day. She focused on Rhys, on the expression on his face, on the way he was often looking at her rather than at the camera lens.

And she saw exactly what her mother had wanted her to see.

She saw the difference between the Rhys in her

photos and the one in the frame in her living room. She saw the difference in his expression. She saw the happiness that she brought to him. The same happiness that he'd always made her feel.

She called her mother back immediately.

"Mom, I know you have to go, but can I just say one thing?"

"Sure, honey."

"I'm a fool."

Her mother laughed. "All scientists must eventually face that which eludes them. Usually, that's right before a grand discovery changes their lives."

"Do you regret giving up your acting for Dad?"

"Yes. But do I regret my life with your father? Not at all. I shortchanged myself, and in doing so I shortchanged your father. You certainly don't need to do the same. I'm sure you can find a way to make your lives mesh into something you'll both be happy with."

13

Dalton's Magic Rule #14:
Reveal all the cards in your deck and be willing to make a
fool of yourself.

With the stage lights shining down on him, Rhys smiled and moved fluidly through the act's closing number. He didn't miss a beat, and the audience was right there with him, a sea of smiling faces that, at least for the night, wanted to believe that life was more than what could be rationally explained. On the inside, he was on autopilot. There was no kick. No rush of adrenaline. No pride that he'd invented over half the tricks in the show.

All he could think about was Melina. He winced inside every time he thought of that last night. She'd done exactly what he'd asked her to do—taken a risk and tried to please him. Yes, she'd gone too far, and she'd been motivated by fear more than desire, but he should have been more careful in pointing that out. Instead, he'd done exactly what her former boyfriends had done—made her feel inadequate. Granted, that hadn't been his intent, but he'd screwed up so bad it's no wonder she'd ignored his declaration of love and gotten on a plane the first chance she got.

Max signaled to him from the right wing, indicating it was time to call the final volunteer from the audience. Rhys nodded, grateful that the end was near. Once the crowd was gone, he'd tell Max what he'd decided. If Melina couldn't stomach living in his world, then he'd have to live in hers. It might be tough at first, but Max was a great magician. If he needed Rhys's help, he'd be there for him, but he was through with touring. He'd already told his parents, who'd offered only their support and well wishes.

He loved Melina. If he had any chance of winning her back, that's what he was going to do.

With Amanda and Tina backed into the shadows downstage, he moved upstage. "Now, for my final trick, I'm going to need the assistance of someone from the audience." Half the audience raised their hands, and Rhys smiled naughtily. "Actually, I should have been specific. I'm going to need a volunteer who's wearing a skirt." Three-quarters of the hands went down. Rhys grinned. "Let's narrow that down even more. A female volunteer who's wearing a skirt."

Several men laughed and lowered their hands.

Max walked into the audience, approached a dark-haired woman, and began leading her toward the stage. "Ah, lovely. Please step right up here, ma'am."

They moved closer, and Rhys narrowed his eyes, straining to see past the glare of the stage lights. He sucked in a startled breath when he recognized Melina. "Melina?" he said, forgetting he was wearing a mic. Her name echoed throughout the theater.

"Yes, it's Melina, everyone." Max helped Melina up the stage steps, then used his own mic to introduce her. "Melina has volunteered to place herself in Rhys's capable hands, so let's give her a big round of applause."

Rhys could only stare at her. Her eyes were like saucers, and her pale skin was flushed a splotchy red. Her legs were bare, and she wore the same high heels she'd worn with the corset, but her light, pale-green coat covered what she wore. With two hands, she gripped the coat closed, as if she feared he was going to rip it off her.

"Honey," Rhys said, no longer caring who heard him. "You don't have to—"

Max led Melina to the center of the stage and, with a flourish, indicated Rhys should get started. When he hesitated, Max sidled up to him, covered his mic, and gritted, "The sooner you do the damn trick, the sooner you can get her off stage. You might want to do that before she passes out."

"Why—"

But Max walked off, and Rhys stepped closer to Melina. She looked at him, her mouth trembling. Then she lifted her chin and smiled, a sweet, brave smile. He reached out and squeezed her hand. She squeezed back. "Do it," she whispered.

Snapping out of his daze, Rhys pulled out his scarves. They weren't the same ones they'd used in Lake Shasta—he'd retired those to his dresser drawer. He showed the audience two white scarves, then knotted them together. Then he turned to Melina. "Ma'am, can you tuck these under the edge of your skirt, please?"

Melina took the scarves with one hand, keeping a death grip on her coat with the other, and awkwardly tucked them under the bottom of her coat. Stooped over, she looked up at him questioningly. Rhys cleared his throat. "Good. Now, can you tell me what color underwear you're wearing?"

Melina's eyes got even wider. "W-why?" she stuttered.

Rhys smiled and turned to the audience. "Smart woman. Always ask questions before you tell a strange man anything about your panties."

The audience laughed, and Melina just stared at him, frozen and silent. They'd never rehearsed this particular trick in front of her, so he told her so she wouldn't be nervous.

"If you tell me what color your underwear is, I'm going to make a scarf of that exact same color magically appear, tied between the two scarves you've got under your skirt."

She smiled. "Really? You can do that? That's amazing."

"I can do a lot of things with my hands that would amaze you."

The audience laughed, but he barely heard them. He and Melina smiled at one another, and for the first time in days, the tension eased out of him.

Things were going to be okay.

Melina straightened, letting the tied scarves flutter to the floor. "Instead of telling you what color my underwear is, can I show you?"

Rhys's eyes rounded. He laughed nervously and jerked his head at the crowd that had suddenly gone quiet. "Honey, I know I tend to make a woman forget where she is, but we've still got an audience here."

"I know," she said. "But I'm making a point." She grasped the edges of her coat.

Rhys reached out to stop her. "Melina, don't—"

She whipped her coat off and dropped it on the floor.

The audience went wild.

From downstage, Amanda and Tina whistled.

From stage right, Max whooped and pumped his fist.

Rhys just stared.

He knew that when he died, hopefully only after a long, full life with Melina, he'd picture her at this exact moment—scared out of her mind, but holding her own, her shoulders back, her chin up, and a challenge in her eyes daring him or anyone else to respond less than positively to her bikini-clad body.

Her smoking-hot, he-wished-they-were-alone-so-he-could-jump-her body.

Damn, he was good, he thought, noting that the black and red polka dot bikini hugged her curves in all the best places.

The audience quieted, and still Rhys didn't move or speak.

Melina narrowed her eyes and peered more closely at him. That's when he realized Melina wasn't wearing her glasses.

"Where are your glasses?"

She frowned. "In...in my coat."

Rhys snatched up the coat and searched the pockets until he found her glasses. Carefully, he slipped them on her nose. She blinked at him. He grinned.

"When you want to make a point, you go all out, don't you?"

"Being in love with a professional magician isn't going to be easy. I have to upstage you every now and then."

"So you're in love with me?"

Melina nodded. "For years."

"Love, as in love, love?"

"Love, love," she echoed.

He dipped his head and kissed her, a reverent meeting of lips that drew an "aww" from the audience. Throwing her arms around him, she buried her face in his chest. "Can we get off stage now?"

"You bet." Rhys turned to Max. "Can you take over here?"

Max strode up to them, hugged them, then turned to the audience. "Talk about a tough act to follow. Now, ladies, who's wearing something that can compete with that bikini?"

The audience roared as Rhys helped her into her coat and off the stage. He ushered her into his dressing room before sweeping her off her feet and twirling her around. His hands immediately wandered inside her coat, and hers followed suit, tugging off his jacket and unbuttoning his shirt faster than he thought possible. She was working the fly of his pants when she suddenly stopped. "Wait. I forgot something."

Rhys groaned. "Can it wait? I'm right in the middle of a performance here."

She giggled and stroked him through his pants, delighting in his groan of pleasure. "It'll just take a second, I promise."

He took a deep breath. "Okay."

"I'm ready to answer the pop quiz now," she said.

Rhys laughed. "Okay," he repeated.

"What would I do to have you?" she reminded him. "That's what you asked me."

"I haven't forgotten. So what's your answer?"

Reaching into her bikini top, she pulled out the small booklet she'd tucked against her breast.

He stared at it. "It's your passport."

"That's right. Now open it."

He did. Stuck in between the blank pages was the paper lizard he'd given her so long ago. "You kept it."

"I didn't answer you before, and I'm so sorry about that. I love you. If you still want me to, I want to be part of your life. I can't travel all the time because I know that won't make me happy. But I don't think that's what will make you happy either."

"So what are you proposing?"

"I propose that we put our heads together and do what we do best."

"Tell me," he whispered.

"What else? We're going to make magic," she whispered back.

EPILOGUE

Dalton's Rule of Magic #15:
The show must go on.

Melina looked up as Rhys walked into the house. He sighed as he put down his briefcase and loosened his tie, everything about him radiating exhaustion. Concerned, she strode toward him. He smiled when he saw her. "Hey, Ladybug."

"Hi, yourself," she said, giving him a hug and a light kiss.

He growled when she pulled away, cupping her head and pressing her close for a longer, deeper set of kisses. Before she knew it, he was backing her into their bedroom and going at her clothes with a determination that made her laugh.

"And here I thought you were tired."

He tsked. "I'm never too tired for this."

Once he had her naked, he laid her back on the bed, smoothed his hand over her stomach, then froze. He leaned in closer, pressing her thighs apart to get a better view. With the lightest of touches, he ruffled the dainty curls that had been shaped into a heart.

"Wow."

She pursed her lips. "That's it? Wow? Do you have any idea how traumatic it is for a woman to get waxed?"

"No." He rubbed her lower stomach in soft, soothing circles. "If it's uncomfortable, then stop doing it." Kissing her stomach, he slowly skimmed his way down to her core and nuzzled her. "But I have to say, this heart's damn sexy."

"Then it's worth a little embarrassment to have it done."

He raised a questioning brow. "Just what happens at these wax places?"

She pushed his head down. "Would you stop talking and get back to what you were doing?"

"Yes, ma'am," he said. As always, he put his best effort forward with magical results.

An hour later, they were lying content in each other's arms when Melina remembered. "Lucy called."

"And?" There was no mistaking the wariness in Rhys's tone.

"She said the dean is bugging her about doing another presentation with Jamie. Apparently, they made quite an impression the first time."

"How fast did she say no?"

"Actually, I was surprised. She said yes. She grumbled about it the whole time, though. She said she's trying to soften the dean up so she'll get some extra grant money."

Rhys snorted. "Soft isn't really Lucy's thing. She's got the hots for the professor."

Melina gasped. "Are you kidding? Lucy and Jamie? No way. That's like...like putting together—"

"What?" Rhys questioned. "A footloose professional magician and a small-town entomologist?"

He tugged on her arm, and she curled back into him. "I suppose anything's possible, but that would be truly shocking."

"As shocking as Max having the hots for Grace?"

"What?" she shrieked. She shoved him away, stood, and slipped into her robe. After tying her belt, she propped her hands on her hips. "Okay, now you're just playing with me."

Rhys threaded his fingers behind his head and shrugged.

"When?"

"The night after you accosted me on stage wearing nothing but your bikini. Grace called the theater to check in with you, and Max answered the phone. I have no idea what was said or if and when they've ever met in person. All I know is that he's been walking around in a daze, muttering her name. He's reverted back to his old ways, nothing like the new-and-improved Maxwell Dalton, magician and host of the getting-to-be-quite-famous Dalton Theater."

Still trying to imagine Grace with Max, or heaven

forbid, Lucy with Jamie, Melina walked to her dresser and touched the little box she'd set there earlier. Smiling wickedly, she decided to wait a little while longer before she gave it to him. "Well, I suppose he deserves some time off for good behavior. Let's not forget we're together because of him."

Rhys snorted. "Let's not forget he's the reason I didn't get into your pants when you were sixteen."

"Like that would have happened." When he stared at her, she smirked. "Okay, it would've definitely happened. But who can blame him for being jealous of you? He felt bad and tried hard to make amends."

Eyes wide, Rhys stood and waved his palm in front of her face. "Hello? This is the same man who copped to taking an ax to Metamorphosis."

Melina smacked his hand away. "Impulsive, but determined. He knew you weren't going to be happy with Seven Seas so he made sure it didn't happen. Then he worked like a madman to get you guys signed at the Portofino Casino. You both did."

"I suppose," Rhys grumbled. "In any case, the meeting with the attorneys to nail down the final contract went well today." He lit up. Rubbing his hands together, he started untying her belt. "Now I get to enjoy the fruits of my labor—at home and in my bed with my own little sex dynamo—while he has to slog through standing-room-only performances in the newest luxury resort in Vegas."

Melina rolled her eyes. "Yes, I'm sure all that fame and female attention will get old eventually." He knelt in front of her, peeled back her robe, and kissed her stomach. She ran her hand through his hair and peered down at him. "Sex dynamo, huh?"

"Hey, you're the one who bought the crotchless underwear and crop. I was just your hapless victim."

She jumped on him and pushed him down at the same time, digging her fingers into his ribs even as he did exactly what she wanted him to. Flipping her onto her back, he covered her with his body and pinned both wrists above her head with one hand. "I love that this is your favorite position," he whispered, then laughed when she tried to knee him. He easily deflected the blow, pushed her legs apart, and rubbed the hardest part of him against the softest part of her.

They moaned together, and he took that as his cue to get busy with his free hand.

"Before you—" She gasped when he sucked her nipple into his mouth, then flicked it with his tongue. Tangling her fingers in his hair, she tugged to get his attention. "Before you distract me with sex, can I ask you a serious question?"

He groaned dramatically and dropped his forehead lightly on her chest. "If you must, but make it quick. I have a wife to satisfy."

"Be honest. Do you have any regrets about leaving the act?"

He sighed then met her gaze. "Just one," he said.

She jerked in surprise, inadvertently rubbing against his erection. He bit back a moan even as he shook his head. "Don't look like that. I love my life. I love our home, love being able to travel with you when we want, love that I get to manage my brother's flourishing career and charge him an obscene amount of money for the tricks that I invent for him. Most of all, I love that I can have all that and you can be happy studying your bugs at UNLV. I love you."

"Then what's your one regret?"

He lowered his head and whispered in her ear.

She smiled. This time when she rubbed against him it was deliberate. "That's okay. That pair of cuffs has bad memories, anyway. Think how fun it'll be to find our new favorite pair." It shouldn't be hard, she thought, given the assorted restraints that now waited on her dresser. But for now, she wanted only to enjoy his touch.

BOOKS BY VIRNA

THE BEDDING THE BACHELORS SERIES
Book 1: Bedding The Wrong Brother (Rhys)
Book 2: Bedding The Bad Boy (Max)
Book 3: Bedding The Billionaire (Jamie)
Book 4: Bedding The Best Friend (Ryan)
Book 5: Bedding The Biker Next Door (Cole)
Book 6: Bedding The Bodyguard (Luke)
Book 7: Bedding The Best Man
Book 8: Bedding The Boss**

HOME TO GREEN VALLEY SERIES
Book 1: What Love Can Do (Quinn)
Book 2: The Way Love Goes (Conor)
Book 3: I'm Gonna Love You (Brady)
Book 4: Best Of My Love (Riley)
Book 5: Because You Love Me (Sean)

SAY YOU LOVE ME SERIES
Book 1: Say It Sexy
Book 2: Say It Sweet

ROCK CANDY SERIES
Book 1: Rock Strong
Book 2: Rock Dirty
Book 3: Rock Wild**
Book 4: Rock Free**

**Coming Soon

BEDDING THE BACHELOR SERIES

Bedding The Wrong Brother
(Bedding the Bachelors Book 1)

Determined to find her inner sex diva, Melina Parker enlists her childhood friend, Max Dalton, to tutor her after hours. Instead, she ends up in the wrong bed and gets a lesson in passion from Max's twin brother, Rhys Dalton, a man Melina's always secretly wanted but never thought she could have.

This #1 Bestselling Contemporary Romance is rated HHH ("Heat, Heart & HEA") and involves a bed mix-up, hot identical twins, sex lessons, naughty word games, light restraint, a shy sex bomb who's afraid she's boring and a playboy hero determined to prove she's got everything he'll ever need.

Bedding The Bad Boy
(Bedding the Bachelors Book 2)

This bad boy is ready to work some magic...

Identical twin and Las Vegas performer Max Dalton has

always been the number one bad boy in his family, and he's appreciated the women and fame that comes along with his reputation.

Grace Sinclair is on a mission when she comes to Vegas, one that involves asking Max, her best friend's brother-in-law, to give her the pleasure no man's ever been able to. She suspects Max has more layers than he lets people see, but she's determined to keep her heart safe even as she offers him her body.

What neither of them plan on is love--or the triangle the media stirs up with Max's blonde bombshell actress friend.

Will Grace see beyond Max's bad boy façade long enough to trust him with her heart? And will Max figure out what he really wants before he loses the one woman who makes him believe in love again?

Bedding The Billionaire
(Bedding the Bachelors Book 3)

Free-spirited Lucy Conrad enjoys her friends but keeps others at a distance, especially her affluent and judgmental family...and the billionaire she once dated, Jamie Whitcomb. Despite their explosive chemistry, experience has proven she'll never fit into his world.

Charismatic Jamie enjoys work, women, and wealth. When duty demands he take over running the family business, he jumps in full-throttle; his only regret is Lucy's refusal to take the ride with him.

Then tragedy strikes and Lucy realizes that in order to gain custody of her orphaned niece, she must prove she can fit back into the high-society world she once rejected. The solution? Accept Jamie's make-believe marriage proposal, and be seen as the type of mother her niece deserves. Respectable. Controlled. Willing to play the game.

With her faux-fiancé by her side, Lucy exchanges dirty martinis and leather for champagne and silk. But when the passion between Lucy and Jamie only grows greater, they have to make a choice: back away from each other and not get hurt...or risk everything for the kind of love money can't buy.

Bedding The Best Friend
(Bedding the Bachelors Book 4)

As the new year approaches, nice girl Annie O'Roarke finds herself bored and lonely. She wants more excitement. More adventure. And more sex...even if it won't be with her secret crush, her best friend, Ryan Hennessey. Annie's determined to be "bad" for once in her life, and that includes completing her "naughty" list in a city where being bad is just an ordinary day: Vegas.

Ryan Hennessey is a firefighter who relishes his time off with Annie. Annie's the only person he can count on and he'd never jeopardize their friendship. Then Ryan discovers Annie's "naughty" list. Although he's stunned Annie is raring to explore her wilder side, he doesn't trust anyone else to keep her safe.

So long as he's there to protect her, Ryan's going to teach Annie the true key to being a bad girl.

A bad girl takes what she wants.

Will Annie be brave enough to act on the passion that sizzles between her and Ryan? And will Ryan convince himself and Annie that love is worth gambling for?

Bedding The Biker Next Door
(Bedding The Bachelors Book 5)

Jill Jones has good friends, a great job, and a steady amount of dates. What she doesn't have is a kinky or wild bone in her body—or so she thinks. Then she meets a handsome tattooed biker who lights her on fire. Suddenly she's saying yes to all sorts of things, starting with a night in bed, no strings attached.

A security expert, Cole Novak protects others for a living, but he's weighed down by grief that he couldn't save the most important person in his life. Then he meets Jill, and for one night she brings color back into his world...only to walk away, plunging him back into the now-familiar darkness.

Soon Cole discovers that Jill is closer than he realized—living in the very house he plans to sell in order to leave the past behind. With the wild woman of his dreams suddenly the girl next door, will Cole still sell the place and move away, or will he soak in more of Jill and open his heart to hope and love?

Bedding The Bodyguard
(Bedding The Bachelors Book 6)

Hollywood actress Kat Bailey is on track to win an Oscar, but in the past year she's been embroiled in a nude photo scandal, threatened by a fan of her cheating ex, and run off the road in what could have been a deliberate act. Now she's renting a cabin in Lake Tahoe, considering the pros of leaving acting—including living a normal life for a change.

Bodyguard Luke Indigo initially turned down protecting Kat because he worried his intense attraction to her could compromise the job. But when he learns Kat has gone into hiding, Luke's sense of duty has him following her to Tahoe. Once there, he pretends to be a vacationing neighbor in order to stay close and protect her. As they spend time together, Luke learns Kat's charm is more than skin deep. She's smart. She's kind. And she's oh so sexy.

Kat's intrigued by the steely-eyed man who exudes danger but touches her so tenderly. Even better, he seems to have no idea who she is, making her think she's finally found a man who wants her for herself rather than her fame.

However, when Kat learns Luke is the same bodyguard her manager tried to hire to protect her, she fears ambition not love has been his agenda all along. Can Luke convince Kat that he'd protect her no matter whether he's hired to or not....and can he convince her that he wants her: body, heart, and soul?

HOME TO GREEN VALLEY SERIES

What Love Can Do
(Home To Green Valley Book 1)

Ireland has always been home for the five O'Neill brothers, but several tragedies, including the recent death of their mother, have them feeling lost. After making an unexpected discovery, eldest son and former rugby player Quinn O'Neill heads to Forestville, California, in the enchanted river valley where his mother grew up. There, he hopes to learn more about his family and explore the possibility of settling someplace new.

Traveling the world before opening her own bakery is Lillian Parker's dream, and she's one step closer to achieving it after winning an internship with a world-famous pastry chef in Miami. Unfortunately, Lillian's mother is pressuring her to stay in Forestville and help run the family B&B. Then a handsome Irishman blows through the door with charm and sex appeal to spare, and suddenly Lillian's not sure what she wants.

Sparks instantly fly, and Lillian finds herself agreeing to show Quinn around the area. Soon their building feelings have them wishing for more time together. But Quinn's just beginning to explore the magic of Green Valley wine country, and Lillian needs to stretch her wings. Even worse, exposed secrets pit Lillian's family against Quinn's, creating thorns in their blooming love.

Can passion survive conflicting family loyalties? And can love bond Quinn and Lillian together forever when dreams of adventure versus home and hearth threaten to keep them apart?

The Way Love Goes
(Home To Green Valley Book 2)

A middle child of five Irish brothers, Conor O'Neill always enjoyed life footloose and fancy free. Then Con's mother dies and he's never felt so lost. With his oldest brother, Con explores new possibilities in Green Valley, California, where his mother grew up. Finding inspiration in the great, wide Pacific, Con opens a surf shop in nearby Timber Cove where he meets the classiest lass he's ever seen.

Madlyn Sanchez is surprised when the Irish surfer seems to take a liking to her. Older than him, a high-strung wedding planner, she couldn't be more different than Conor. But the two have one thing in common—they're both looking to start over. Before Madlyn knows it, they kick off an unlikely, passionate romance. But when

Madlyn's responsibilities in San Francisco can no longer be ignored, she kisses Con goodbye and wishes him well.

Missing Madlyn more than he ever thought possible, knowing he's let one too many opportunities pass him by, Conor closes up shop to go after her. In San Francisco, however, he discovers the truth behind Madlyn's real life—a child and an ex-husband still in residence. Con just learned to commit to one woman—can he commit to a child as well?

In no time at all, mother and son have Conor's heart. But can an Irish rogue who once cherished his freedom convince the love of his life he's more than ready to put down roots while still teaching her to fly?

I'm Gonna Love You
(Home To Green Valley Book 3)

Steadfast and pragmatic Brady O'Neill, second eldest of five Irish brothers, never thought he'd leave Dublin. But after the death of his daughter and his parents, and the loss of his wife, Brady realizes he can no longer live in the city where he experienced his greatest joys and deepest heartaches. Moving to America, he joins his brothers in Forestville, California, to open a family restaurant. What he doesn't expect is the spark he feels when he meets Anna Kincaid, a confident, gorgeous woman with enough sass to sink a ship.

Owner of a local eco-adventure tour company, Anna Kincaid is familiar with all that is Forestville. So when recent Irish arrival, the insanely handsome and sexy Brady O'Neill, wants to visit the vineyard where his mother grew up, she agrees to be his guide. Soon, Brady's showing his appreciation with more than flirtatious smiles and mind-boggling kisses.

The chemistry between them may be explosive, but tensions heighten when Anna's recklessness puts her in danger. Brady's lost too much already; and a risk-taking woman with an impetuous nature could cost him yet again. Will Brady risk giving all he is to Anna? And will Anna learn that there's no greater excitement in the world than taking a chance on love?

Best Of My Love
(Home To Green Valley Book 4)

Irish charmer Riley O'Neill never thought he'd fall for one woman so soon after moving to America. After all, his brothers were all about love and commitment these days, and *someone* had to keep the ladies satisfied. However, after months of keeping Erica Underwood in the friend-zone, Riley has a decision to make—continue to enjoy variety, get back together with his ex-girlfriend in Ireland who's wanting a second chance, or finally make his move on Erica, the one woman he can't get out of his mind.

After a short holiday in Ireland, Riley returns to California wine country and suddenly he's treating Erica different. Teasing glances and lingering touches indicate he's ready to be more than friends, but Erica's worked hard to get over her crush on Riley. She's started seeing another man and when Riley finally declares his feelings, she's convinced he's only attracted to the challenge she now represents.

But Riley's not giving up on Erica, and he sets out on a mission to prove they're perfect for one another, in bed and out. Soon, they're inseparable, and their passion burns wild and hot. Until a phone call from Riley's ex Lucy threatens to destroy everything…

Will Riley and Erica crumble in the face of unexpected challenges, or will their love bring out the best in both of them and lead them to happily ever after?

Because You Love Me
(Home To Green Valley Book 5)

Readers have fallen in love with the Irish O'Neill brothers…now it's time for Sean O'Neill's story!

Sean and his four brothers moved from Dublin, Ireland to California wine country. One by one, the O'Neill brothers have fallen for the women of their dreams. Now it's Sean's turn, and he's determined to convince Juliana Madison, his college English professor, that he's not just a younger man—he's definitely the man for her.

Now that classes are over, will Juliana play it safe or will she give in to her attraction to the brown-eyed Irish lad whose tender words and strong arms fill her with joy and make her believe in love again?

SAY YOU LOVE ME SERIES

Say It Sexy
(Say You Love Me Book 1)

This life I'm relishing--the women, booze, and parties-- won't last forever. But while it does, I'll take it all in with no regrets. Pleasure stands paramount. When I party, I forget all the trash that's happened in the past. It's the same when I'm acting, when I become someone else, someone not afraid to feel or make others feel. It's what I live for: The next party. The next role. The next girl.

That's my life. That's the way I want it to be.

Except now I've met Gwen...

Garrick Maze, young Hollywood's hottest bad boy, just landed the male lead in a new network television series. Known for indulging in wild parties, casual hook-ups, and fast cars, he spends his days on set and his nights on the town. Love's the last thing on his mind, especially when it comes to his ice queen female lead.

Gwendolyn Vickers intends to be America's next celebrity sweetheart and that means keeping her public image pristine. The last thing she needs is to be linked to trouble-making heartthrob Garrick Maze. But he's shamelessly flirty and sexy as sin. Her body craves him. Soon, so does her heart.

When secrets from the past clash with the bright lights of fame, Gwen realizes there's more to Garrick than washboard abs and sex appeal. He'll prove that when it comes to mixing mind-blowing pleasure with true love, he's not about to let her down.

Say It Sweet
(Say You Love Me Book 2)

Outwardly, Erica Ellis seems to have it all. At twenty-three years old, she's already hit the *New York Times* bestseller list and her breakout novel is being made into a network television series. But even after collecting her cushy advance for Book 2, she can't seem to forget the struggles of her past or stop longing for the sexy and sweet man who views her only as a friend.

A former fighter turned actor, Shane Mason hides his pain behind a good-guy façade just like he hides his growing feelings for Erica. The willowy blonde is way out of his league…or so he thinks, until an unexpected hookup at a party has him thinking he and Erica might just be perfect for each other.

Only it turns out Erica doesn't remember the night they spent together. Now Shane has a choice—walk away or let Erica see all that he is and can be to her: a nice guy and a bad boy. A friend, fighter, and lover.

ROCK CANDY SERIES

Rock Strong
(Rock Candy Book 1)

I've seen and done it all--sex, drugs, rock-n-roll, and then some. I've made the cover of Rolling Stone. I've won Best Rock Performance at the Grammy's. I'm living a life of fame, wild tours, crazy money, and insanely hot women. But the one woman I can't get is prim and proper cellist, Abby Chan--gorgeous, natural, talented as all sin. The first time we met, I knew we would be something special. She's not convinced, but I am.

Now I'm going to prove she's all the woman a wild man like me will ever need...

Liam Collier, sexy and enigmatic frontman for Point Break, the world's hottest rock band, is at the top of his game. With two songs in the Billboard Top 10, he's a rock-and-roll bad boy, known for his trademark falsetto as well as his proclivity for partying and hooking up with gorgeous women. For Liam, falling in love was something he figured would happen far off in the future--not on the first day of his first world tour. And not with his super sexy but extremely reserved background cellist.

With a Master of Music degree from Juilliard School of Music, Abby Chan is on the road to becoming a cellist for the New York Philharmonic Orchestra. But to pay back her expensive education, first she has to travel another kind of road--a gig playing cello for the North American leg of a garish rock band's world tour. She'd expected hard work and long hours, but what she never expected was the intensity of her reactions to Liam Collier. He's sweet. He's hot. And despite being surrounded by roadies and the world's most beautiful women, he's set his sights on her.

When classical music meets rock and prim propriety meets a carefree attitude, Abby and Liam venture outside their comfort zones. What they discover is that living wild is the perfect preparation for flying high--on love.

Rock Dirty
(Rock Candy Book 2)

As one of the hottest drummers in the world, Tucker "The F***er" Benning lives life hard. But when his band's world tour is cancelled, Tucker finds himself stuck in an airport with no destination in mind...until he spots a red-headed knockout hurrying through the airport on her way to Paris, France. She's classy, sexy, and turns heads. Why not buy a first class ticket and follow her? That's when the real fun begins.

Dominique "Nikki" Lorenz, heiress to her mother's magazine empire, is headed to Paris, hoping to leave behind her celebutante tabloid reputation and make a new name for herself. She's amused when the famous Tucker Benning sits next to her and starts flirting—could he *be* any more of a rock star? But when he presents a naughty proposal, she figures why not have one last wild experience before settling down?

Once they land in Paris, though, Nikki makes a stand—no more naughty stuff. She has a fresh and clean reputation to build, and being seen with Tucker won't help. Yet Tucker's bad boy allure is impossible to resist and so is his softer side, which makes her feel cherished and worthy.

Tucker has a decision to make—does he fight for his band, or does he commit to the woman he's come to care about, a woman who longs for love and stability his rock star lifestyle can't give?

Tucker's life has always been about fame, fun, and f***ing around. But now Nikki needs him and he'll do whatever it takes to win her heart...including fighting dirty. Because love is worth risking everything.

ABOUT THE AUTHOR

Virna DePaul is a *New York Times* and *USA Today* bestselling author of steamy, suspenseful fiction. Whether it's vampires, a Para-Ops team, hot cops or swoon-worthy identical twin brothers, her stories center around complex individuals willing to overcome incredible odds for love. Bedding The Wrong Brother, which begins the Bedding The Bachelors Series, is a #1 Bestselling Contemporary Romance and a USA Today Bestseller.

Virna loves to hear from readers at www.virnadepaul.com.

CONTACT VIRNA HERE
Website: www.virnadepaul.com
Twitter: @virnadepaul
Email: virna@virnadepaul.com
Facebook Fan Page: www.facebook.com/booksthatrock